Barrett Wendell

Stelligeri and Other Essays Concerning America

Barrett Wendell

Stelligeri and Other Essays Concerning America

ISBN/EAN: 9783337404116

Printed in Europe, USA, Canada, Australia, Japan

Cover: Foto ©Andreas Hilbeck / pixelio.de

More available books at **www.hansebooks.com**

STELLIGERI

AND

OTHER ESSAYS CONCERNING

AMERICA

STELLIGERI

AND

OTHER ESSAYS

CONCERNING

AMERICA

BARRETT 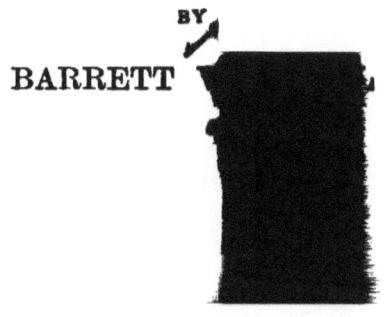 BY

IN

STELLIGERORUM

Memoriam

They came in youthful ardour here, where we
  Follow their footsteps.   Here like us they played
  And worked ; like us had follies, that dismayed
Their shaven elders.   Hence exultantly
Like us they encountered life, eager to see
  Its prizes theirs.   Unperfect, brave, they made
  Our poor world better.   Like them, unafraid,
May we at last merge in eternity.

From out their old New England, still pure
  Of foreign taint, where in their dreamy past
    They stand heroic, comes the courage now
    That nerves us for the conflict we must know.
What nobler prize for who the trial endure
  Than place in their companionship at last ?

Harvard College, 1893

CONTENTS

		PAGE
I.	STELLIGERI	1
II.	THE FOUR AMERICAN CENTURIES . .	21
III.	SOME NEGLECTED CHARACTERISTICS OF THE NEW ENGLAND PURITANS . .	45
IV.	WERE THE SALEM WITCHES GUILTLESS ?	63
V.	AMERICAN LITERATURE	91
VI.	JOHN GREENLEAF WHITTIER . . .	147
VII.	MR. LOWELL AS A TEACHER . . .	203

I

STELLIGERI

STELLIGERI

I

A FEW years ago the authorities of Harvard University made in their quinquennial catalogue a change which has generally commended itself to modern good sense. For the first time they wrote it in English. Changes in this catalogue have quite as much precedent as uniformity. Only ten years before, the quinquennial catalogue had been a triennial. And they say that no two numbers had ever possessed quite the same characteristics of form and arrangement. But until 1890, all these official lists of those whom Harvard College—or Harvard University, as nowadays they prefer to call it—had educated or honoured, had in common one trait that is now definitely a thing of the past. They were written, from beginning to end, in something that passed for Latin.

No doubt there was obvious absurdity in officially naming an every-day Yankee Johannes or Jacobus; or in translating such abnormal Christian names as that of Increase Mather into barbarous terms like Crescentius. The absurdity of similarly Latinizing surnames—an absurdity discarded ever so many years ago—was no greater. No doubt, equally, the long strings of incomprehensible Latin abbreviations which used to follow the names of distinguished alumni were very ridiculous. But to many of us the absurdity seemed lovably harmless; and with it went one or two phrases that some of us are sorry to lose.

Chief among these, perhaps, was the sonorous little sentence that used to close the numerical summary of Harvard men. The total number was given first; then, formally subtracted from it, came the number of the dead. In the class lists the names of the dead were prefixed by asterisks. In the final summary, the number of the dead was defined thus: *E vivis cesserunt stelligeri.—They that bear the stars have passed from among the living.* One did not read the sentence often. Some of us looked at it so seldom that I have heard it honestly misquoted in a far more dogmatic form: *Ex his stelligeri in cœlum processerunt.—Of these they that bear the stars have passed forth into the heavens. Stelligeri* was the fatal word. To all of us who cared for the old catalogues, the dead men of Harvard were always *stelligeri—they that bear the stars.* And some of us had a sentimental way of looking at the skies of a clear night, with a half-phrased feeling that their faint, twinkling, lasting glory had something to do with our college mates who were gone before us. For did not the catalogue say so ? It was a pleasantly childish fancy which made those who yielded to it sometimes feel more akin than usual to the old worlds of youthful humanity which the colleges and universities once kept so much in mind. I have not had the heart to look for what our dead men are called now—"deceased," perhaps, or "no longer living."* At all events, they are no longer *stelligeri*,—which I am informed, by the way, was never classical Latin.

The change came none too soon. Harvard College, to be sure, has always been true to what remains its oldest and strongest tradition—that every man and every generation has an inalienable right to think. Thereby the men and the generations make their conclusions—no matter how orthodox—impregnably their own. The deep conservatism which has preserved this heretical tradition for above two centuries has resulted in a good many superficial changes meanwhile. The first conclusion arrived at by people who do their own thinking is generally that their immediate predecessors have been seriously mistaken. And the Harvard of one generation has almost always been a perceptibly different place from the Harvard of the next. The unparalleled growth of the college during the past twenty years, however, has made the most marked change in its history.

* Since writing this I have looked, and find them "Reported as deceased."

The old graduates—*stelligeri*—belonged to classes
small enough and submitted to systems of instruc-
tion similar enough to make them in a sense all
friends, with a hundred traditions and memories in
common.   Nowadays, when every Freshman class
is bigger than the whole college was fifty years ago,
and when every man meets the elective system at
the college threshold, everything is altered.   One
cannot say for the worse : most of us who know
modern Harvard well think it a far better place
than the old.   But it is not the same.   We have
discarded no end of useless things and phrases ;
we have introduced no end of useful ones ; we are
striving to know and to preserve the truth with
as much eagerness as any who have gone before.
In every superficial way, though, our experience
is utterly different from that of our elders.   The
authorities might have kept the old forms.   They
might have called us, in our time, *stelligeri* too.
But we could never have been the real thing.

II

A TYPICAL evidence of what the real thing was
lately came to me.   A kinswoman on her death-
bed sent me as a farewell greeting the record of
his class which her father, dead these thirty years,
had kept from admission to college until the end of
his life.   It is in a small, leather-bound note-book,
with thick, old-fashioned leaves.   It begins with

an alphabetic list of the class as they entered college. A series of simple hieroglyphics indicates who attained the supreme glory of the Porcellian Club, who belonged to the Hasty Pudding, who to the Phi Beta Kappa, who dropped out of college, and so on. Then come pages of notes as to the professions the men took up, whom they married, how many children they had, and in general what became of them; then pages into which are pasted clippings from the newspapers, generally eulogistic and frequently obituary. The last bears a date forty-eight years after graduation, and only a few weeks before the faithful recorder died. He did not live to see his college jubilee.

Provincial, even trivial, these records may seem. If I remember rightly, the most eminent of all the fifty or sixty men they concern was one who for a few years became a sober local dignitary. They tell little of character, anyway, beyond the fact that a rather surprising number of the class seem to have been afflicted with insanity or insane wives. In cold blood, one cannot call the little volume much more than a record of names and dates. And yet I have seen few books which affect me as less prosaic. These dry records were kept unremittingly for above half a century by a loyal Harvard man who longed to have always before him every little fact that transpired about the college and the college men of his time. In substance, they were almost as formal as the firm, slow handwriting in which they were traced. In essence, one felt, every stroke of the fine pen was loving.

The men these records concerned were almost all native Yankees of the old stock. In later life by far the greater part of them were honourable and useful citizens—divines, lawyers, physicians, merchants, teachers. It is some years now since the last survivor died. Every one, I think, was written down *stelliger*.

There was little time to send an answer for this gift. Yet I tried more than once to phrase an answer that should tell all it meant. Finally, in despair of expressing the thing literally, I tried to make some verses; that effort, it seemed, might tell more than any formal phrases of the emotion I had to convey. The verses, though rather lame and halting, served their purpose. My kinswoman sent back word that they were welcome. She had loved the old Harvard traditions, too. At her death, a few weeks later, it was reported that she had bequeathed to the college, in memory of her father, a small foundation for an annual lecture on the immortality of the soul.

III

THE verses thus written I have used for the dedication of this little book. That they were made

for so widely different a purpose is one reason
why I have liked to use them here. The essays
of which the book is made were written indepen-
dently, with no thought of collection, and little
that they had anything in common. It was only
when they were all done that I began to see how
they belong together.

The reminiscences of Mr. Lowell were written
first. When he died, people did not half appreciate what his professional work as a teacher had
been. So I wrote down what I remembered of it,
as the best tribute I could pay his memory. At the
time I did not sign it, because at such a moment
the obtrusion of an unknown name seems to me
impertinent. What any reader cared for was not
who might have written this tribute, but what the
tribute might add to those already paid the memory of a man who had lived to be the unques-
tioned head of American letters. That objection,
I think, need not stand in my way now. In substance, the paper belongs with the others ; and in
a collection of one's own work, it would be silly to
assume one's self unknown in such sense as must
be the case when one's occasional writing chances
to be accepted by an established magazine.

The other papers in this book are all occasional,
in the conventional sense of the word. They
were written to be read or presented at formal
meetings. In 1891 I was asked to tell the American Historical Association as much as I could

read in twenty minutes of what I thought about the New England Puritans. A little later I was asked to address the meeting held by the Essex Institute, at Salem, in commemoration of the two hundredth anniversary of the issuing of warrants against the witches. In the autumn of 1892 I was asked to address the Public Schools of Worcester, on the four hundredth anniversary of the Discovery of America. A little later I was invited to give a formal lecture on American Literature at Vassar College. And when Mr. Whittier died, the American Academy of Arts and Sciences invited me to write the memoir of him for their Proceedings.

Some such statement as this was almost necessary, to explain the differences of form and manner among these papers. One does not write for school children in quite the way that one falls into when addressing a learned society ; and one's personal reminiscences can hardly be phrased in such style as one unconsciously assumes when making a university lecture. These natural divergences of style and temper, then, made me at first think of these papers as separate things. Then, as I turned them over, I began to see that among them they had gone far to express, from different points of view, certain opinions about American life, past and present, that I was glad to have formulated. In collecting the papers, however, I was not sorry that their style is not uniform. Its very irregularity will go as far as anything can to disclaim the assumption, which always seems inherent in print, that one's views are final. What I have written here is only what I have grown to think during thirteen years of academic teaching—a mode of life dangerously remote from practical experience, but perhaps more favorable than that to observation. What I have said is shown, by its very diversity of form, to be only an expression of what an individual who has little to do with active life has come to think.

IV

In brief, it seems to me that the America of the past resembles, in more ways than one, the *stelligeri* of Harvard. It is a thing we shall not see again; we love to think about it and to cherish its traditions; and if we drop love—using our heads and not our hearts—we find it on scrutiny not altogether so imposing as we like to imagine it. For it was not divine but human; and the only thing that can make humanity godlike is unviolated tradition.

In a certain sense, we may say that hitherto the history of America has been that of a great national inexperience. This does not mean, of course, that human life has not existed here in all its real complexity. It means that hitherto

our communities have generally been so far from
overcrowded, and our people so free to make their
way whither they would and could, that in
America the material problems of life have presented themselves less regularly than in Europe.
So hitherto we have been naturally disposed on
the one hand to over-estimate small merit and
petty success, and on the other to display our
vices in forms which, however deplorable on a
moral scale, still have in them something of
youthful naughtiness as distinguished from ma-
ture rascality.

The race to which these generations of inexperience were coming met them with a dogmatic
creed actually based on such experience of human
frailty and wickedness as must always be the lot
of any dense society. Creeds long survive experience. The dogmas of Calvinism were uttered
for generations in communities where, in normal
moods, they could not seem exhaustively true.
A certain unconscious divergence between state-
ments and facts followed, as a national characteristic. It grew until our freer minds flung the
old dogmas away, trying to make new and better
ones of their own.

The new dogmas, which in brief rest on the assumption that human nature is perfectible, are a
great deal more inspiring than the old that harp
so on depravity. What is more, they are a good
deal more true to the national inexperience of

America than were the old ones. But they have
been uttered, and are uttered still, by the descendants and the heirs of a race that for generations has been habituated to the most serious kind
of assertion unchecked by reference to actual fact.

On the optimism that underlies these new dogmas is really based our tremendous national
faith in democracy. If human nature is really
perfectible, even though it never get to perfection,
democracy can really solve the problems of life,
when they come upon us in all their force, as
they have never been solved before. But if
human nature should after all prove damnable,
democracy may turn out a less certain panacea
than we have been accustomed to believe.

Experience nowadays seems bound rapidly to
supplant the national inexperience that has hitherto been our most characteristic heritage. As experience grows about us, there is reason to doubt
whether the serenely optimistic dogmas of the last
century or more are essentially so true as we have
been taught at school. There are moments, in
fact, when the gloomier dogmas that the Calvinist
fathers brought from wicked, overcrowded England seem after all nearer the truth visible to our
own eyes. And in that case democracy cannot
seem as ultimate a solution of life as it used to.
There are obvious aspects in which it is beginning to look terribly like the substitution of a
myriad damnable tyrants for a few.

V

So much, in one way or another, the papers in this little book will show. Coldly written down here, it looks disheartening, if not disloyal. Yet I do not think that it is really either. It is disheartening only if we are afraid to face a future of manly struggle instead of Utopian dreams. It is disloyal only in the sense in which a subject is disloyal who feels bound not to deny the sins and the vices of a sovereign he willingly serves.

To any thoughtful man, I suppose, the evils and the dangers of his own time are often more apparent than its nobler traits. And, very surely, this is no depressing symptom. So long as evils and dangers are recognized, they will be met, at least, with effort. It is the hidden disease that works the worst havoc. And even when these evils and dangers seem to permeate a whole national system, there is no need to lose courage. Human institutions, like human beings, must have their faults and their weaknesses. They must be transitory. Even the great religions of the world are bound to change and to pass; much more, the political systems by which from time to time men submit to be governed. But through every change runs what after all is a steady purpose. Really, in its deepest heart, the human race is constantly struggling onward in a blind effort to be happier, wiser, better.

Any man or any generation can see only a momentary fragment of this struggle. In that moment, however, men can perceive the forces that they must meet and conquer if they are to leave their children a richer, wider heritage than they themselves received. To meet and to conquer these hostile forces they must yield themselves up to human leaders; and these human leaders, being human, must be frail. Now it is a sovereign man whom the loyal are bound to follow, again a sovereign class, with us a sovereign people. And how hearty, for all our misgivings, is our real loyalty to our sovereign, we can all feel for ourselves when our blood tingles at the thought of submission to domination. We may lament as we please the follies and the errors of the thousand-headed populace who stand for us in the place traditionally held in history by consecrated sovereigns. But each of us would still rather live and die a citizen than even the proudest subject. Whoever does not feel this spirit in himself cannot know, in his inner heart, what the name American means.

VI

THERE are moments, however, when the sight of the great changes that are now coming upon us makes our hearts sink. If America in the future, we tell ourselves, were to be like America in the past, all would surely go well, as far as human foresight can reach. There is none of us, I believe, who would not willingly trust our future to such native guidance as has governed our past. But the floodgates are opened. Europe is emptying itself into our Eastern seaports; Asia overflowing the barriers we have tried to erect on our Western coast; Africa sapping our life to the southward. And meantime the New England country is depopulated, and the lowlands drained by the Mississippi are breeding swarms of demagogues. And so on, and so on, and so on. If the future were to be as the past, we say!

Well, how if it were? Better still, how, after all, if perhaps it be? In many ways it will inevitably differ. Its experience must be far sterner, far fiercer — in every way on a grander scale. But if the evils to meet be greater, may not greater virtues rise to meet them? For, after all, as we scrutinize this past, we cannot find the facts quite so splendid as the traditions. A little while ago we tried to sum up our impressions of what this real past was; and we called it no better than two centuries or so of national inexperience, youthfully asserting human nature to be essentially better than scrutiny shows it to have been even on the spot where these cheerful generalizations were made. That the past was not really all that we like to boast, is a fact that should give us courage. By the same token, it

may well be that the future shall not bring all
that we dread to fear.

VII

It is posterity, of course, that makes traditions.
But it can make them only of the stuff it finds
ready. The children in their youth know the
fathers, in their age tell their own children what
manner of men the fathers were. Untrue in a
thousand details, then, traditions — like other
ideals—are bound to rest on a basis of truth perhaps deeper than appears to one who coolly
scrutinizes in all their living confusion the facts
from which they rise.

Petty we may find the realities of our actual past
—sordid, inexperienced. But whatever these realities, we all know, and instinctively we all thrill
with the knowledge, that from that past have
come the traditions that have guided and that
still guide our native national life. What the
reality was, after all, is not the chief question.
More notable for us, a thousand times, is the
ideal which that reality, with all its errors, has
transmitted to posterity. For that ideal, that
tradition—smile at its details as we may—is really
noble. It is pure, simple, aspiring. In us all it
has bred the deepest feeling that marks us as fellow-countrymen. Let us be pure in heart, simple
in life, aspiring in effort. Then so far as in us

lies we may transmit to our children an enriched heritage of such tradition as the fathers have left us.   Our faults, like theirs, shall fade and pass ; our memories shall merge with theirs in the dreamy past from whence shall come the inspiration that shall make greater than our own America the unseen America of the future.

VIII

It is easier to realize such sentiments as this in small instances than in large. We are right, then, in cherishing so dearly our local traditions, our family pride. We are better men, I believe, and better citizens, for loving not only our country but our States, not only our States but our towns, not only our families but our colleges. And very surely there is for some of us no firmer warrant that the traditions we love shall live as long as our memory shall last than the warrant we find in remembering the *stelligeri* of Harvard.

Their lives and their notions were often petty enough, limited, absurd to their children as the barbarous old Latin catalogues will probably seem to ours. There were plenty of weaklings among them, too, no doubt. Almost every class had its Tom who drank himself to death, or its Dick who was justly jailed, or its Harry who proved the most deplorable of husbands. Nor were these *stelligeri*, as a body men, of great distinction. They number several thousands, and among them are not many dozens who, as the years begin to pass, can survive in human memory. Names and dates most of them must ultimately be. The rest oblivion.

Yet whatever their personal traits, there has come from them to us who follow them a tradition of our own without which we, and our country, were poorer. Like the great traditions of America, this little tradition of Harvard is pure, simple, aspiring, and lasting. And in it finally merge all the folly, the error, the weakness, the nonsense of the swiftly passing college generations that for two centuries and more have received and preserved it. On the open books of the college shield is the single word, " *Veritas*"—" *Truth*." Keep truth in view, say the silent voices of them that bear the stars, and trust, like us, that all shall be well.

In aspect, in thought, in phrase, in purpose, we of the present and the future differ more and more from them of the past. That their names were preserved in pompous, barbarous Latin, and that ours shall be recorded in plain, every-day English, typifies the difference with a truth that makes the very change a preservation of the deepest tradition of Harvard. But in spirit, if we be loyal, we may be at one with them. And so far as our parts may go to preserve for America what is best, to discard what is evil, to fight our fight bravely, and at last to go without misgiving to our rest, our way is plain before us. For we have only to follow the footsteps of them that bear the stars.

II

THE FOUR AMERICAN
CENTURIES

(An Address before the Public Schools of Worcester,
Massachusetts, on Columbus Day, October 21, 1892.)

THE FOUR AMERICAN
CENTURIES

I

AMONG the most interesting books of the past
year is Mr. John Fiske's "Discovery of America."
It is a history of that fascinating kind which tells
us, to be sure, little that was not known before-
hand ; but that shows us, so simply that we
hardly realize we are being taught, where each
scattered bit of knowledge belongs. Careful
students of one period or another may find in
Mr. Fiske's work errors of detail : to write so com-
prehensive a book without minor errors were almost to transcend human frailty. But no one, I
think, can read the book without a fresh and a
lasting appreciation of that great process of
human development whose most significant moment we celebrate to-day.

For, after all, the moment when Columbus set
foot on the unknown land which marked the limit
of the western seas is a moment worth all the honour
we pay it, not for its own sake, but because it was
no accident—no isolated thing ; it was one step
in a great process, started in the most remote past

and even as yet unfinished. In itself it might
have meant as little as the landfall of those half-
legendary Norsemen who have left behind them
no more trace than the winter tales of their sagas.
But the landing of Columbus means more : it is
significant to all men, as a part of the direct process by which human beings finally came to know
the inevitable limit of material things.

II

As I write that phrase it sounds mysterious.
Yet what it means, any child, who will stop to
think, can understand. Wherever we read of
human beings in history, up to the time when
this Western continent was discovered, we find
that they were living in a world surrounded by
oceans or countries they knew nothing about.
The Romans, for instance, knew most of Europe
pretty well, and they knew something of Asia
and of northern Africa. But all about them,
north, south, east, and west, the earth stretched
on, they knew not whither. Somewhere in the
Western Ocean there was an *ultima Thule*—an isl-
and beyond which no man had gone. And there
were faint legends of other great islands to the
west of Gibraltar, and of a fabled Atlantis, no
more tangible than the rivers and canals of the
planet Mars. And just as those imperial Romans
—in so many ways people quite as civilized as the

earth has ever known—lived in a world where beyond known lands and seas there stretched on an
endless region of lands and seas that were unknown ; so, in just such a world of endless possibilities beyond its known limits, lived every
human being, recorded or unrecorded, until the
process of discovery was finished which the voy-
age of Columbus began.

It is worth our while, then, to consider for a
moment just what this change in our knowledge
of the shape and limits of the earth means.   In
order to live, human beings must be fed ; in order
to be fed, they must cultivate and consume the
fruits of the earth.   And as population anywhere
increases, more and more of the earth has to be
cultivated to feed it.   In this very city of Worcester, for example, there was probably a time, not
quarter so long ago as the time of Columbus, when
everybody who lived here could raise on his own
land enough food to supply himself and his family.   At this moment, though Worcester is not a
great city like New York or London, it is a good
deal too large to be supported by food grown on
Worcester soil ; it has to send West for its beef
and its flour, and so on.   What is more, I should
be surprised if there were among you many who
do not number among your friends somebody
who, instead of settling down at home, has gone
West ; in other words, somebody who could not
find at home work that would provide him with

such food and clothing and comfort as he had made up his mind to have, and who has gone to a newer country in search of a quicker fortune. Now just such a process as each of you can understand here on a small scale, is always going on all over the world. The places where people live grow too crowded to support them; so people move somewhere else where there is more room.

I do not mean that people in general sit down and quietly think this out. In the time of Columbus, for example, I do not suppose that many people in Europe actually realized that the time was not far off when Europe would be overcrowded. But, all the same, the fact was there; and with it the fact that no human being, until long after Columbus was dead and buried, knew whether there might not be, beyond the known world, endless lands where the human beings who should by and by be crowded out of Europe might go.

Now think of what every one of you knows today. On this globe of ours, which any of us might easily travel around in three months, there are two great continents—one in each hemisphere; and there are some islands in the Southern seas, Australia and New Zealand, and a great archipelago of smaller ones; and that is all. There is nowhere else where human beings can ever go. When the population of the world, as we see it mapped in any school geography, has increased in anything like the proportion in which, within less than a hundred years, the population of the city of Worcester has increased, the human race will have such a problem to solve as in all its history it has never had before. It will be face to face with what it can already foresee—with the limited power of this earth to support life, or, to use the more mysterious phrase with which I began, with the inevitable limit of material things.

III

In the time of Columbus, four hundred years ago, the Old World of Europe was getting far nearer its own limits than anybody realized. I do not mean, of course, that it was within a few years of starvation ; such processes as I am now talking of move on, not by months or years, but by centuries. This four-hundredth birthday of the New World might better be called the fourth birthday of the whole world. But even before the time of Columbus, the more active men in Europe were getting restless; the spirit of exploration was in the air. Travellers had forced their way eastward across the whole width of the continent of Asia. Sailors had begun to round the southern limits of Africa. And all this meant that, hardly knowing what it did, growing Europe was calling to its aid the resources of the Indies. Had there been no Indies, or had the lands which Columbus always believed to be Asiatic proved to be anything other than the coasts of a new hemisphere, almost untenanted by man, then—even by this time—the final struggle of European humanity with the inevitable limit of material things might have begun.

For, after all, looked at in a larger way, we of America are Europeans as truly as our language is English. There are differences, to be sure, between us who have crossed the western seas and our kinsfolk whom our crossing has permitted to remain safely at home. Such differences, with that fine instinct of self-respect which is, perhaps, our finest national trait, we love to cherish, much as we love to cherish family pride. But just as our past history is as truly European as is the past history of Spain or of England, so is the future history of Europe bound to include our future history too. For this world we live in we know now to be a whole world, united in itself as surely as it is eternally separate from other planets and other systems. Its history is bound to be the history of the domination of that race which in the struggles of the ages proves most worthy to survive. And that race, I hope and believe, is the race of which we form a part and in a certain sense the advance guard—the race whose great records were first written, now by this nation, now by that, in the history and the literature of Europe.

IV

To this history and this literature our New World has added its own pages. To-day we turn the fourth; what shall be written on the fifth and those which shall come beyond, none of us may ever live to know. And to prophesy were idle. But it seems to me that we may well consider for a few moments the record that our New World has already made; and perhaps pause for a little while to consider also its meaning. The limits of the centuries of world history are as accidental as the limits of the years in a man's life. Our birthdays are matters of chance. But just as each of the years which are carrying us on from cradle to grave has for each of us who looks back on it a character of its own, so when we look back on the four centuries that separate us from the time when to our forefathers all beyond the western sea was fathomless mystery, it seems to me that each of the centuries begins to grow distinct.

V

THE first—the Sixteenth Century of the Christian era—sums itself up in our American history as the century of exploration and of Spanish conquest. In the records of that time there is nothing, I believe, more fascinating than the maps. Almost year by year, as fresh navigators brought back fresh reports, we can watch the islands and the continents emerging from the fantastic mystery of legendary seas. Perhaps no one feature of this growth is more notable than that of the region to which German geographers first gave the name of the maligned Florentine, Amerigo Vespucci— a name, as at last we know, that in every sense we may be proud to bear. Sailing to the southward of the lands where Columbus had preceded him, he came upon another land, seemingly independent of those, hitherto unknown. In the older maps it appears as an island, of which the exact limits are still to be fixed, much as Greenland used to appear in the school geographies of my childhood. Map by map these limits grow distinct, until by and by we see that the first America of Vespucci was no island at all; it was that easternmost part of our own great continent to which later geographers finally gave what had once been the legendary name of Brazil. And as map by map the continent grows, we can watch the emergence into human history of these northern regions, which were destined to be the homes of our fathers and our children.

During the first century of our Western history, however, these northern regions were little vexed by other than exploring Europeans. It was to the southward that Europeans were making their

permanent mark, in the regions that still bear
the name of the Indies, and those yet wider regions
which to this day retain an impress that could
have been made only by the imperial Spain of
Charles V. and Philip II. Within our own country, one may almost say, the only lasting mark
of that century is the name Virginia, preserving
for us the memory of her who, until our own
time, might stand unchallenged as the noblest of
English queens. Beyond our limits, in Mexico,
in Peru, in the Indies, Spain wrote upon the face
of the New World the ineffaceable records of a
system in devotion to which untold millions of
earnest lives have been and shall be spent; a system which assumes that all earthly authority must
come straight from God in Heaven, through his
temporal and his spiritual anointed.

VI

THE second century of American history—the
Seventeenth Century of the Christian era—is one
whose records mean far more to us. In the course
of it, I believe, all but one of the colonies were
finally settled which were destined to be the germ
of the United States; and those which for a little
while owned the sovereignty of Sweden and of
Holland yielded themselves to the authority of
the English crown. For all that to the north of
us the subjects of Louis XIV. were striving to

gain for France such a foothold as to the southward the subjects of Charles and of Philip had
gained for Spain, it is with no lack of confidence,
I believe, that we may name the second century
of American history the century of English conquest.

It was the century in which the English planters
were finally settled on the James; the century
in which the Pilgrim fathers came to Plymouth
and the Puritan colonists to Boston Bay. Our
national records are full of traditions which belong to this epoch. It was the century of Captain
John Smith and Pocahontas, of Peter Stuyvesant
and the old Dutch worthies of the Hudson, of
Miles Standish and Governor Winthrop, of Roger
Williams, of King Philip's War, of Sir Edmund
Andros, of the Salem witches. In the country
towns of New England there is hardly a burying-
place whose gray stones do not bear the names of
men and women who have been resting beneath
the pines and the elms since the days were still
fresh in memory when our own forefathers broke
the soil that is still ours. But it seems to me
that too few of us are disposed to remember
what, as the centuries begin to pass, stands out
as the chief record of that olden time. It was
in the Seventeenth Century that first were planted
in American soil the seeds of the system which,
whether we know it or not, is the system by
which our national life must stand or fall. In

that century our continent first gave asylum to
the race which, in its heart of hearts, acknowl-
edged and still acknowledges no earthly authority above the common law.   For, looked at in the
light of the centuries, our own constitution and
all that has grown up beneath it are but out-
growths, strong with the strength that comes
from natural, undistorted growth, of that firmest
known system of human rights—the common law
of England.

VII

THE third century of American history—the
Eighteenth of the Christian era—is a century of
which the memory is still more our own.   From
whatever point of view one looks at it, no fact in
its course is much more salient than the American
Revolution.   To foreigners and to superficial ob-
servers, the chief trait of this great event seems
perhaps to be that for the first time in modern
history it demonstrated the power of colonies to
break free from the control of a mother country.
To us, I think, it has a trait more notable than
that : it marks the beginning of our conscious national life; it gives us a right to name this third
century of American history the century of native
conquest.

Between this century of native conquest, however, and the two centuries of foreign conquest

3

which preceded it, there is a distinction, I think, which, unlike in themselves as were the conquests of England and of Spain, groups them together; and which marks our native conquest as a thing apart.   The purpose of the conquests both of England and of Spain was to impose upon a new world, hitherto untrodden by civilized men, the systems of government which had prevailed in old Europe.   It was the purpose of our native conquest to impose no system on anybody or on any territory; but only to maintain, in the face of all the military force of England, those rights which by the common law of England not even the English crown had a right to touch.   This is the trait that distinguishes our revolution from all the others that have since troubled the Old World and the New.   One and all, these have striven to substitute for some old, established authority, some brand-new system, devised by enthusiasts and untried by mankind.   Ours, and ours only, strove not to innovate, but to preserve; not to manufacture a ready-made system of law and government, but to guard and protect in its normal growth a system of government which had been proved sound and wholesome by centuries of ancestral experience.

As our glances at American history come nearer to our own time, their field perforce grows narrower.   As I think of this third century of our history, I find myself recalling to memory two structures on the Atlantic sea-board which together symbolize much of the history we have considered.

The first is on the Island of Cape Breton. On a little peninsula there, rocky, grass-grown, dotted with grazing sheep — a little peninsula which stands between the everlasting surges of the foggy ocean and a quiet harbor still capable of floating a navy—is a great line of ruined fortifications. About the middle of the last century, a whole regiment of British sappers and miners worked for half a year in the endeavor to blow them up and obliterate them. Yet all this work has only made huge breaches in the walls, and half-filled the ditches at their foot. Grass-grown, deserted but for the sheep and a few poor fishermen and smugglers, the walls of Louisbourg still remain indestructible in their outline. You or I can still trace there every bastion and every port. And this useless, deserted ruin, permanent in its defenceless strength, is almost all that remains on the eastern coast of North America to symbolize the power and the fall of that system of authority which France, with the example of Spain before her eyes, once hoped to impose upon our whole continent.

The second structure is nearer home. In the straggling village that has grown at the mouth of the Piscataqua, is a fragment of an old, unpainted wooden house. Newer houses and village shops crowd close upon it now. But even in its shabby

decay its great gambrel roof and its two square
chimneys preserve a dignity of their own. It is a
dignity less austere, less stern, less lordly than
that of the lasting masonry of Louisbourg; but
a dignity still far above that of the cottages and
the shops of later times. Here in his day lived
William Pepperell, the Yankee merchant who, in
the name of King George II., took command of
the Yankee volunteers. From this house he set
forth, leading them against that fortress of Louisbourg, where, behind the strongest military architecture of France, the system of authority had
intrenched itself to withstand and to oppose the
growth of that other system whose strength lay
in the English common law. And hither he returned, victorious with his undisciplined Yankees
over the trained mercenaries of Louis XV.—to
be made, in honor of his good fortune, the one
native baronet of New England.

In honor of his good fortune, I say, because
whoever reads the story of that first Yankee conquest must admit that our victory came half from
the blunders of the French and half from pure
chance, hardly at all from any skill or notable prow-
ess of our own. In a way, I think, that very ele-
ment of chance, of good fortune, makes the conquest of Louisbourg all the more typical of the
growth in America of that system whose strength
lies not in force but in law.

But Sir William Pepperell's house is to-day as

far sunk from its high estate as is the fortress of Louisbourg itself.   Here the American Revolution has done its work.   When he set out against Louisbourg, Pepperell stood for that force which characterized the second century of American history as opposed to the force which characterized the first.   Thirty years later, his descendants, unchanged in principle, found themselves opposed, not to the past but to the future.   The victorious people of America had scant mercy for whoever opposed them.   The Pepperells, like hundreds of other loyal gentlemen, saw their lands confiscated and themselves driven into lasting exile.   And to-day strange villagers swarm over what were once their gardens and in the dismantled chambers of their dismembered house.

In this aspect, it seems to me, the ruinous mansion symbolizes, more clearly than we like to admit, the state in which the American Revolution left us.   In that great struggle, I believe, the Americans were in the right, and in the right because what they fought for was no abstract principle, but rather the maintenance of their vested rights.   In so doing, however, they were forced to be for the moment rebels.   As rebels, it was their inevitable misfortune to find opposed to them that great part of the best and worthiest people in the land who in any crisis feel bound to throw themselves on the side of established authority.   And this old gray house of the Pepperells, deserted for a

century and more of all who have had a birthright to be there, typifies what few of us allow
ourselves to remember—the tremendous sacrifice
of good men and true that was the inevitable
price of our national independence.

VIII

NATIONAL independence—that is the substance
of the fourth and last page of our American history, the page we are closing now, with the Nineteenth Century of the Christian era. The days of
the Spanish conquests are past; of English conquests, too, and of native. For a hundred years
we have held in our grasp the prize that the Old
World proved all too weak to retain. What account shall we give of it ?

Our greatest national characteristic, it seems to
me, is a superb self-confidence, born at once of
temporary freedom from limits and of necessary
ignorance of standards. We have had the territory of a whole continent wherein to make our
experiments and to correct our blunders. And
we have never had close at hand any older and
wiser nations than ourselves by which as a people
we might measure our own shortcomings. It has
been the fashion, then, very honestly to assert
that God opened for us of America a clean page
of history, and that the record which our free-
born citizens are writing there is a new one in the

history of mankind. At times it has seemed so to all of us. There is a great charm in those high-sounding commonplaces of triumphant democracy that we have borrowed rather from the impracticable philosophy of Eighteenth-Century France than from the sane experience of England, Old and New. There is a certain æthereal purity in the philosophical utterances of our own New England which sometimes seems very marvellous to those of us who would be helped to live in the spirit. And we are far enough to-day from that terrible conflict which has knit together this Union with bonds closer than before it men dreamed of, to see that North and South alike had ready, when the moment came, endless armies of men who would lay down their lives for what they deemed the truth.

But this is not all the story. We must admit, too, I fear, that we have in our history records as sordid, as corrupt, as debased as any that the Old World can show. We must admit that as this continent, which a century ago was a hardly explored wilderness, grows densely populous, the human nature that is bred here is the same old human nature of the ages. We have added incalculably to the material wealth of mankind; we have added perhaps a few exquisitely pure notes —none the less pure for their faintness—to that literature which our mother tongue has for a thousand years been adding to the literature of

the world; we have tried on a scale never attempted before the great experiment of democratic self-government. And, when we honestly
begin to give an account of this new page of human history we have tried to write alone, we are
forced, I think, to say that there is in it no new
lesson. The law of life decrees that life shall be
an unending struggle. Relax the limits of material things, as for us they have been awhile relaxed, and the struggle grows less intense. But
faster and faster, as the human race fills the earth
whose limits we know at last, the inevitable old
struggle for existence is upon us, with all its old
possibilities of heroism and of baseness.

Whether we will or no, then, the future offers
to us of America little else than it offers all mankind. As our past history is European, so our
future history must be shared with all the world.
And we may feel sure that whatever form it take,
the grand outline of that future history must be
the same as the grand outline of human history
through all time. The life of man is an unending struggle for existence, now with the material
things about him, now with his own kind. Our
fathers were fighters; we must fight ourselves;
and the battle must be passed on and on to our
children till latest time.

IX

THE final question, then, for us of America to ask ourselves, is whether in our own history we can find ideals and figures that shall serve us and our children for watchwords in the struggle. There are moments when the materialism, the baseness, the corruption that at any moment mark human existence anywhere, make one sick at heart. The dominant fact of our national history, too, the fact of democracy, is sometimes terribly disheartening. For, with all its splendid generosity to the people at large, democracy at heart must always be the sworn foe of excellence. No man can excel without making other men seem less in comparison. And whatever tends to inequality, without which no excellence can be, arouses the spirit of democracy to fierce rebellion. By the side of the great histories of the world, then, this page of ours, despite its material records, seems none too rich or noble in those traits which make mankind better.

But, for all this, and for all the blatant patriotic untruth that sometimes makes one feel as if all patriotism were a lie, we may find in our records traits and figures that, if we prize them well, may guide us in the struggle to come as surely if not so brilliantly as any in the records of peoples who more willingly recognize and respect superiority.

The trait that above all others, I believe, we of the United States should reverence and cherish and preserve is the trait that phrases itself in the angry phrase of any country Yankee—"I'll have the law on him." Other people would fight foul; we fight fair, or strive to. In our deepest political nature there still lurks the spirit that our forefathers brought from England two centuries ago; the spirit—so much misrepresented since— that fought and won the American Revolution; the spirit that, discarding all cloud-spun theories, declares and with self-restraint maintains the final authority of that common law which, disdaining empty philosophies, has maintained and extended through the centuries those privileges and rights which the sure teaching of human experience has shown us may safely be permitted to men.

And if we ask what figures we may place before ourselves, as incarnations of what is best in our national history, I find myself more and more apt to answer that there is in our history a roll open to all eyes, in which those who ponder upon it may well feel more and more pride. It is not a roll of great men—rather, perhaps, of petty politicians, some of them a bit contemptible to those who knew them best. Better still, it is a roll of native citizens called by a process that almost fatally excludes the higher excellences of character, to stand for a little while before the eyes of the world. I mean the roll of the dead Presidents of the United States. At a moment like this it is not fitting to speak of the three* who still survive. But when their time shall come, these men, I believe, could ask in human history for no worthier place than that which shall be theirs. For their stations await them in the lengthening line of those sovereign representatives of a sovereign people, for no one of whom that people has as yet the right to feel a blush of shame.

* Written before the death of Mr. Hayes.

III

SOME NEGLECTED CHARACTERISTICS

OF THE

NEW ENGLAND PURITANS

[A paper read before the American Historical Association at Washington, December 30, 1891 ; and published in the *Harvard Monthly*, April, 1892.]

SOME NEGLECTED CHARACTERISTICS

OF THE

NEW ENGLAND PURITANS

I

On February 15, 1728, the Reverend Benjamin Colman, first minister of the Brattle Street church, preached the Boston lecture in memory of Cotton Mather, who had died two days before. Cotton Mather had lived all his life in Boston; there is no record, they say, of his ever having travelled farther from home than Ipswich or Andover or Plymouth. Of sensitive temperament, and both by constitution and by conviction devoted to the traditions in which he was trained, he certainly presented, to a degree nowhere common, a conveniently exaggerated type of the characteristics that marked the society of which he formed a part. But Benjamin Colman, at least in earlier life, was of different mettle. After graduation at Harvard College he had passed some years in England, at a time when clever Dissenters could see good company. In Boston, whither he had returned late in 1699 to take charge of the new church subsequently known as the Brattle Street, he had been so liberal—at least in matters of discipline—as to impress the Mathers, who were the leaders of the strictly orthodox party, as a dangerous Radical. It is not too much, perhaps, to say that his ministerial career marks the beginning of that movement in the Boston churches which, a century later, became Unitarianism and put Calvinism, at best, hopelessly out of fashion. In view of this, his lecture on Cotton Mather becomes curious.

His text is the translation of Enoch: "And Enoch walked with God, and he was not, for God took him." From these words he draws inferences that enable him to expound the career and character of the patriarch, with edifying precision, to the length of four closely printed pages. But what he chiefly insists on is that Enoch's blessed fate

" must be resolved into the good pleasure of God, His wise and sovereign will; and to be sure it was not for any merit or desert in Enoch's holy walking with God. Enoch deserved to have died for his sins as well as any before or after him. . . . Elias was a man of like passions with others. . . . It was not due to the righteousness of either that they were taken without seeing death. Before that God formed them in the belly he designed them their translation."

In other words, the Boston divine, who at times seems the most Radical of his generation, feels bound, as a matter of course, to begin his eulogy on the most distinguished of his fellow-ministers by an assertion in the most concrete terms of the doctrine of election.

II

BEYOND question this doctrine was never, for many hours, absent from the mind of Cotton Mather, nor often from that of Samuel Sewall, the two worthies of the period then drawing to a close whose diaries are best preserved. Beyond question, too, these men were, in this respect, not peculiar, but typical of their time. There is hardly a figure in the first century of Boston history whose conduct and opinions can present themselves, to modern temperaments, as comprehensibly human, unless we keep this doctrine constantly in mind ; and keep it in mind, too, not as a verbal dogma, but as a living reality. It is worth our while, then, to recall exactly what it was.

In the beginning, the Puritans believed, God created man, responsible to Him, with perfect freedom of will. Adam, in the fall, exerted his will in opposition to the will of God. Thereby Adam and all his posterity merited eternal punishment. As a mark of that punishment they lost the power of exerting the will in harmony with the will of God, without losing their hereditary responsibility to Him. But God, in His infinite mercy, was pleased to mitigate His justice. Through the mediation of Christ certain human beings, chosen at God's pleasure, might be relieved of the just penalty of sin, ancestral and personal, and received into everlasting salvation. These were the elect; none others could be saved, nor could any acts of the elect impair their salvation.

All this is familiar enough. What puzzles posterity about it is how so profoundly fatalistic a creed could possibly prove a motive power strong enough to result not only in individual lives but in a corporate life, that was destined to grow into a national life, of passionate enthusiasm, and of abnormal moral as well as material activity.

To understand this nowadays we must emphasize a fact generally neglected by the writers of New England history: namely, the test by which the elect could be recognized. The test of election, the Puritans believed, was ability to exert the will in true harmony with the will of God—a proof of emancipation from the hereditary curse of the children of Adam; whoever could at any time do right, and want to, had ground for hope that he might be saved. But even the elect were infected with the hereditary sin of humanity; and besides, no wile of the Devil was more constant than that which deceived men into believing themselves regenerate when in truth they were not. The task of assuring one's self of election, then, could end only with life.

III

COLMAN, in his funeral lecture, states this doctrine very specifically :

" To walk with God means, in all the parts and instances of a sober, righteous, and godly life, and constancy therein all our days. We walk with God in a sincere, universal, and persevering obedience to the written Word and revealed law of God ; and blessed are the undefiled in the way that walk in the law of the Lord. To walk is not to take a step or two, nor is it for a day or a year, but for the whole life, all our days. We must walk and work while the day lasts ; the light is given for this. How much .does it concern us, then, to ask ourselves whether we have indeed begun this walk with God and to Him ? Whither are we going ? What are we doing ? How do we live and act ; and what will become of us a few days hence ? Will God take us ; take us on the wings of angels and in their arms to His own presence and glory ; or will death drag us out of the body and devils take us away to their abodes of darkness and of fire unquenchable ? " ·

The Puritans themselves would probably have told us, as their lineal religious followers sometimes tell us to-day, in both cases with perfect honesty of intention, that this specifically asserts the duty of man to give himself up to God, with no other purpose than to advance God's glory. Such a statement does not explain in modern terms why any living man ever really did so. Few facts, indeed, seem much truer to

modern minds than that human beings do what
they do not want to do only when some humanly
overpowering motive makes self-denial, in the
end, the line of least resistance. And looking
at Colman's teaching in a modern spirit we may
see in it, without much trouble, an appeal to
an everyday human motive which goes farther
than most things else to explain the apparent
inconsistency of Puritan doctrine and Puritan
character. In short, what ho does, and what all
the Puritan preachers do, is to assume the doctrine of election ; to declare the test of election
to be ability to walk with God, to exert the will in
true harmony with His ; and then, by every means
known to their rhetoric, to stimulate in every
one of their hearers the elementary and absorbing
passion of curiosity, concerning self-preservation.

IV

In the diary of Cotton Mather, a most characteristic Puritan document, this trait appears in
a form almost incredibly exaggerated. We have .
in these manuscripts a pretty full account of him
from eighteen to sixty-one. The number of
private fasts he kept was enormous. It is not too
much to say that they were at least weekly throughout those forty-three years. For twenty-two of
those years he habitually held vigils, too,—all-
night watches in his library of ecstatic prayer and
effort to penetrate the veil that is between God

and man. And this was but a little part of his
passionate effort to walk with God. And the
only modernly comprehensible motive to account
for all this passion is the one he records in a self-
examination at the age of forty-two :

"I am afraid," he writes, "of allowing my soul a wish
of evil to the worst of all [my enemies]. . . . Q.
Whether the man that can find these marks upon himself
may not conclude himself marked out for the city of
God ? "

The same trait appears in Increase Mather ;
the same in that vastly less emotional personage,
Samuel Sewall ; the same reveals itself distinctly
in almost every godly portrait in that quaint
gallery of worthies that fills so much of Cotton
Mather's " Magnalia."

V

THIS book, with all its obvious faults and
errors, remains, on the whole, the chief literary
monument of New England Puritanism. It has
been rather the fashion, of late years, to criticise
it as a modern historical document ; as a record of
actual fact. As such it is certainly untrustworthy
from beginning to end. So modern critics are
generally disposed to put it aside as worthless,
and incidentally, to apply the same adjective to
its author. Psychologically, however, the "Magnalia" is a document of such historic value that
an earnest student of Puritan New England can-

not safely neglect it.   Any work of serious literature, we are beginning to see, must inevitably
express, at least in its implications, the conditions
of the society wherein it was produced. And these
it often expresses in a conveniently generalized
form where they may be better studied than in
individual phases from which posterity, as best it
may, would draw what it is apt to think more
accurate, because more conscious, inductions.
This is the aspect in which the " Magnalia " is
most significant.   As a piece of literature it possesses two traits which should follow directly
from the fundamental self-curiosity of the Puritan character.   Within arbitrary and rigidly defined limits it is intensely imaginative ; and it
displays throughout a serene disregard for that
fine adjustment of phrase to fact which our
modern scientific spirit of veracity assume sfor
the moment to be eternally the chief of the
cardinal virtues.

VI

To understand the peculiar nature of its intensely imaginative quality we may best, perhaps,
refer not to itself but to the passage from Colman's funeral discourse to which we last directed
our attention. The quality is so constant among
the Puritans that you may find it almost anywhere.

" Will God," he writes, " take us   .   .   .   on the

wings of angels and in their arms to His own presence
and glory ? or will death drag us out of the body, and
devils take us away to their abodes of darkness and of fire
unquenchable ? "

This sounds commonplace enough, nowadays.
But a gentleman who once visited Goethe at
Weimar, has told me that Goethe's first question was whether it were a fact that in America
there were still people who believed in actual
winged and crowned angels; and that when
he answered, as was then true, that he believed
in them himself, Goethe looked at him with an
expression he can never forget and exclaimed,
" *Das ist wunderbar !*" Which exclamation, my
friend says, began his emancipation from Puritan
anthropomorphism. To come nearer our own
time, it is not a dozen years since in a Boston
newspaper somebody wrote in a very serious obituary notice concerning a secretary of the American
Board of Foreign Missions, that " few men on
entering heaven will find a wider circle of personal acquaintance or a larger number of those
under indirect obligations."

These things all go together : Colman's angels
and devils, the material angels of the American boy of 1830, the white chokered old mis-
sionary receiving in staid social formality the
emancipated spirits of the Polynesian elect, and
the godly ministers and magistrates of our Puritan
Plutarch. In earlier and later forms they are

concrete examples of the way in which the faculty
we call imagination, exerting itself for generations within the limits of what after all was an intensely anthropomorphic creed, will first create
for itself concrete images, only less material than
the bronze and marble ones iconoclasm casts
down ; and then, while denying that bronze or
marble can be symbolic, will passionately and
honestly assert its own images to be real. Nowadays we are apt to look on all these images—
material and immaterial alike—as only symbols.
But Cotton Mather at least once was rewarded, in
ecstasy, by an actual vision of an angel—wings,
robes, crown, and all ; and there is no reason to
question that Colman, who was well on with his
preparation for college at this moment of Cotton
Mather's highest ecstasy, actually believed his
devils to be waiting, with hoofs and horns and
tridents, for such of humanity as the unspeakable
free grace of his just God had not undeservedly
released, with Enoch, from the ancestral penalty
of human sin.

When Cotton Mather drew his godly portraits,
they stood for figures so vivid in his imagination that he had no more suspicion of their
actual truth than of the elements of fiction
and invention which a modern eye detects in his
God, his angels, his devils. When Colman spoke
of "abodes of darkness and of fire unquenchable," he spoke of something that to the Puritans

represented a fact as concrete as the Tower of
London, or as the George II of whom in the same
lecture he writes thus :

"What an honor should we account it if our earthly
prince would allow us to walk after him in his garden?
Only a few select and favorite nobles have the honor
done them."

And it is not a little significant of the exhaustion
of human power that must follow constant, over-
wrought intensity of exercise that Colman failed
to remark the strict incompatibility of darkness
and unquenchable flames.

To consider this exercise of imagination in another and more modern spirit, what it amounted
to was this :   Only by incessant assurance and re-
assurance that the will was exerting itself in
harmony with the will of God could the insatiable
curiosity to know whether God's free grace were
ours be for a moment stayed.   God's way of contemplating things heavenly, earthly, infernal,
belongs to that class of perceptions to which so
many modern thinkers give the convenient name
unknowable; it is a thing which, true or false,
can never be verified by either observation or experiment.   But the God of the Puritans, for all
he was a spirit, was a white-bearded spirit, with
limbs and passions,—still " *le père éternel de l'école
italienne*," who had made man in His visible image.   To them His will in regard to all things,
great and small, was a thing not only that might

be known, but—if life were to possess any mean‧
ing—that must be known; and that being known
must be proclaimed.   In the intense, incessant
effort that followed to formulate the unknowable
in concrete, anthropomorphic terms, imagination
exhausted itself.   What we call the prosaic color‧
lessness of Puritan life is merely external.   The
subjective life of the Puritans was intensely,
passionately ideal; blazing with an emotional
enthusiasm constantly stimulated by the unrec‧
ognized impulse of selfish human curiosity.   If
you want proof of it, ask yourselves how otherwise
people who after all are not far from us in years
and in blood could have survived the discipline
and the public devotions which were to them
what meat and drink are to the starving.

VII

THE difficulty that followed these godly emo‧
tional debauches is obvious.   To the Puritans the
concrete images thus created in moments of
abnormal ecstasy were more real and unspeakably
more important than any facts of actual life.   Yet
these images, in each case inevitably the creation
of a single brain, could neither be confirmed by
any general process of human observation, nor
tested by any general process of experiment.
Each seer could tell what he himself saw; that
was all.   For the rest, these visions were such

as human language has only metaphoric terms to describe. The consent that governs the meaning of words demands, for precision, wide identity of experience. We all know the insidious temptation to impressive inaccuracy of statement which besets whoever has had a solitary adventure with a fish or a snake. Spiritual experiences are inevitably solitary. Inevitably, too, they cannot be precisely described. Given these truths, given the fundamental errors of human nature, given too the passionate Puritan conviction that an exact account of spiritual experience is the only valid evidence you can give of your eternal salvation, and you get two pretty obvious results.

The first was never better phrased than by Increase Mather, perhaps the most canny of the Puritan divines whose career is recorded. In early life he habitually recorded the heavenly afflations that rewarded his ecstatic prayers.

"As I was praying," he wrote once, "my heart was exceedingly melted, and methoughts saw God before my eyes in an inexpressible manner, so that I was afraid I should have fallen into a trance in my study."—"In his latter years," adds Cotton Mather, writing of him, "he did not record so many of these heavenly afflations, because they grew so frequent with him. And he also found . . . that the flights of a soul rapt up into a more intimate conversation with heaven are such as cannot be exactly remembered with the happy partakers of them."

The second appears very clearly in what Colman wrote of Cotton Mather, with whom in his day he had waged fierce fights :

"But here love to Christ and His servant commands me to draw a veil over every failing ; for who is without them ? Not ascending Elijah himself, who was a man of like passions with his brethren, the prophets ; and we have his mantle left us wherewith to cover the defects and infirmities of others after their translation in spirit. These God remembers no more, and why should we ? and he blots out none of their good deeds, and no more should we."

Nil de mortuis nisi bonum, in other words, is God's will—and not merely a Latin apothegm. In other words still, it is God's will that the whole truth should never be spoken.

VIII

THE traits thus hastily specified are incessant activity, within rigid limits, of anthropomorphic imagination, strained to the utmost by life-long efforts concretely to formulate the unknowable ; and a sense of veracity weakened at once by incessant dogmatic assertion of unprovable fact and by constant conviction that only such truth should be spoken as was agreeable to the disposition of God. These traits appear throughout the "Magnalia." And whoever does not recognize in the "Magnalia" an image not to be neglected of the Puritan character can never seriously understand the Puritans. These traits, as we have seen, both follow directly from unquestioning acceptance, in its most concrete form, of the doctrine of election at a time when its freshness had not faded into theological tradition.   Doubts assailed the Puritans often enough, but, like Increase Mather, the Puritans met doubts not by reasoning—" it puts too much respect upon a devil, to argue and parley with him, on a point which the devil himself believes and trembles at "—but by "flat contradiction."   And the energy that, during the first century of Boston history, fortified them to contradictions as incessant as temptations, sprang, we may believe, from no mystic cause, but from nothing more marvellous at bottom than the almost incredible stimulus which acceptance of this fundamental doctrine gave to self-searching, self-seeking curiosity.

IX

In discussing these old New Englanders one is apt to speak as if, historically, they were a unique class.   It is perhaps worth while, then, for one who cannot profess to be a trained student of history, distinctly to disclaim any such elementary error.   Human affairs, people think nowadays, are as much questions of cause and effect as any other phenomena observable by science.   Similar conditions will produce similar characters anywhere.   And this old hierarchy of ours will very probably prove more like than unlike the other hierarchies that by and by serious students will have studied comparatively. In none of them, any more than in this, will such fundamental traits as we have tried to detect prove to be the sole ones. In no serious study of corporate character can the serious student for a moment forget, for one thing, the crushing, distorting influence of those petty material facts to which we give the convenient name of every-day life. And certainly these concrete facts are generally more profitable subjects of study than such subjective matters as we have dealt with here. What is more, of course, such extreme traits as we have touched on characterized chiefly the leaders — the clergy, the priestly class. During the first century of New England history, however, the influence of this class can hardly be overstated. And just because the concrete facts commonly engross professional students and makers of history, it sometimes seems that such aspects of history as we have glanced at—aspects that in this case reveal themselves with startling distinctness to an unprofessional explorer of Puritan records—have been perhaps unduly neglected.

NOTE.—The passages from Colman are cited from "The Holy Walk and Glorious Translation of Blessed Enoch." (Boston: J. Phillips & T. Hancock, 1728.) The other citations are referred to authorities in my "Life of Cotton Mather." (New York: Dodd, Mead & Co., 1891.) From this is taken directly the account of the Puritan creed.

IV

WERE THE SALEM WITCHES GUILTLESS?

[A paper read before the Essex Institute, Salem, Massachusetts, on February 29, 1892.]

WERE THE SALEM WITCHES GUILTLESS?

I

WITHIN the past few years, I have happened, at the suggestion of friends interested in Psychic Research, to observe three different phases of occult phenomena. The first is materialization, a process by which professional mediums pretend to call up the visible and tangible bodies of the dead. The second is trance-mediumship; the medium, in this case also professional, pretends to be controlled by some departed spirit who uses the tongue of the medium, rather unskilfully, as a means of communication with living beings. The third is automatic writing; in this, acting as a medium myself, I have held a pencil and allowed my hand to run unwatched and uncontrolled by any conscious act of will. I have thus written a great many distinct words, and a few articulate sentences.

Remote as this statement may appear from a confession of capital crime, and far from conclusive as my limited observation and experiment must be, I found that when, in studying the life

5

of Cotton Mather, I was compelled to examine the history of Salem witchcraft, my own occult experiences had induced in me a state of mind that led to some speculative conclusions widely different from those commonly accepted. These I shall venture to state, wholly aware that I-have neither the scientific nor the historical learning necessary to give them even a semblance of authority, but hoping that they may, perhaps, prove suggestive of a line of study which, in more competent hands than mine, might lead to interesting results; for I am disposed to believe not only that in 1692 there was existent in New England, under the name of witchcraft, a state of things quite as dangerous as any epidemic of crime, but also that there is, perhaps, reason to doubt whether all the victims of the witch trials were innocent.

To explain this statement, I may best, perhaps, begin by briefly recounting my own observations and experiments, and then turn to some of the evidence in the witch trials. By comparing this with my experience and with a few facts admitted nowadays—such as the phenomena of hypnotism—I may indicate why I am disposed so heartily to dissent from the rationalistic view of the tragedy of two centuries ago, which has been so admirably and honestly set forth by standard historians.

II

My own observations of modern occultism were made in the order in which I have named them. I saw the materialized spirits first; later I visited a trance-medium; and not till some time later did I try my hand at automatic writing.

Materialization impressed me as indubitable fraud from beginning to end. You went into a room which was subsequently so darkened that you could not discern the hands of your watch. In this dim light, a small company, mostly ardent believers, were wrought up into such emotional excitement as could be awakened by hymn tunes played on a common parlor organ; and presently uncanny shapes began to flit about. Sometimes these emerged from a cabinet in which the medium had professed to go into the trance-state; sometimes they apparently rose through the floor; at least once—to all appearances—they took shape on top of an ordinary three-legged table. These figures would talk with you, would shake hands with you, would sometimes be unpleasantly affectionate in demeanor, and would often end by "dematerializing"—that is, by suddenly flopping down into nothing, much as figures in the pantomime disappear through trap-doors. You could not see how the trick was done, but the trick was essentially like what any number of travelling magicians perform.

Before long, however, you remarked that the habitual frequenters of these unedifying exercises seemed fervently to believe in them. I remember once finding at my side an elderly man who passionately embraced a male spirit that appeared, and returning to his seat whispered to me in agitated tones that it was his son, who had lately killed himself. The son had been a friend of mine ; and when I told the father so, he begged the medium to recall him, that I might speak to him myself and be convinced. But the medium professed inability to recall that particular spirit at the moment, so I was forced to remain sceptical of everything but the fervent belief of the heart-broken father. Next you remarked that, knaves and charlatans as the mediums seemed, they seemed knaves and charlatans of a specific kind. There was no doubt in your mind that they lied to you and tricked you, but I for one could never feel satisfied as to how thoroughly they were aware of the exact extent of their falsehood—as to whether beneath all this nonsense and rascality there were not lurking some mysterious subjective experience that had to them a semblance of fact. Finally, you felt a growing sense of debasement in such surroundings. The uncanny insincerity of the mediums, the crass superstition of the believers who formed the circle, the meaningless words and conduct of the materialized spirits—never indecent, but always petty, trivial, low—led me by and by heartily to agree with a friend who declared that while he did not for a moment believe these were spirits at all, he had no shadow of doubt that if they were spirits they were devils.

The chief trance-medium I visited was a woman of high respectability, and of great apparent sincerity of character. In her normal condition she professed complete ignorance of what occurred when she was in the trance-state. Into this state she could throw herself at will. Once in this state she assumed a voice and manner totally unlike her own, and professing to be controlled by a spirit, she gave you any number of messages from departed friends, whom she sometimes described and sometimes named. In a sitting with her of some two hours I remarked that, in a vague kind of way, she seemed to follow my line of thought. For example, she made a queer noise that reminded me of the death agony of a friend some time before. This recalled him to my mind, and the circumstances of his death. By and by, she named him, and described him with some approach to verisimilitude. The correspondence between what I knew and what she told me was never exact enough to convince me of anything extraordinary; but it seemed close enough to warrant me, if I had believed in mind-reading, in classing her performance as mind-reading, once for all. At the expiration of some two hours, I

found myself obliged to request her, while still in
the trance state, to bring the sitting to a close.
At my suggestion, then, and not of her own accord, she endeavored to resume her natural condition. The result was unexpected: she had a
startling fit. Amid the contortions which accompanied what she asserted to be the departure of
the spirit which had controlled her, she fell on
her knees with a cry of terror, and clutching me
begged me not to let *it* take her away; and she
looked with every appearance of agonized alarm,
at an empty corner of the room from which she
shrank away; you would have said she saw the
Devil himself waiting for her. In a very short
time she resumed her natural condition, at first
rather dazed, and declared that she had no idea
whatever of anything that had happened since
she first went into the trance-state two hours before.*

The most remarkable thing to me about her
was that in her normal condition she was the sort
of person whom you instinctively believe to speak
the truth. It was perfectly easy to assert that
she was a common trickster; but to my mind, at
all events, the assertion was by no means convinc-

* It is fair to remark here, that a friend deeply interested in Psychic Research questions the accuracy of my
memory in this case. I can reply only that the incident
was unique in my experience, and so horrible as to produce
a very lasting impression.

ing. My own impression was strongly that she was an honest person, in a very abnormal state, honestly self-deceived ; and in this abnormal display and in this self-deception was a quality of debasement, more subtle, less tangible, than I had found in materialization, but, if you granted the supernatural hypothesis at all, equally diabolical.

A year or two after this I found that if, pencil in hand, I left my hand free to run as it would, and occupied my eyes and thoughts with other matters, my hand would clumsily scrawl first queer tremulous lines, then letters, then words. This experience was in no wise peculiar. The friend who first directed my attention to these experiments had made a considerable collection of automatic writings from various people ; and these had in common a trait that mine shared with them. The avowedly unguided hand would make for a while—sometimes day after day—apparently meaningless lines that constantly repeated themselves. In time, these lines would grow more definite. Finally a word would be written ; and by comparing a number of the writings you could trace what looked like a long series of almost impotent experiments, finally resulting in this distinct achievement. The first word my hand thus wrote was " sherry."

That it was going to write " sherry " I had no idea. To this point I had been incredulous that it would actually write anything at all. "Sherry" once written, I began to feel more interest in what it might write next. And then soon followed an experience that determined me to give the matter up. In the first place, I found that experiments in automatic writing left me in an irritable nervous condition for which I can find no better name than demoralized. The whole fibre of character seemed for the moment weakened ; will, intelligence, self-control, temper, were alike inferior things after the experiments to what they had been before. In the second place, I found that very soon I could not be quite sure whether I actually let my hand run unguided, or whether I slyly helped it write. And whenever that doubt arose in my mind, there always came with it so strong an impulse to deny its existence, to assert that I had no idea what I was about, that I found myself for the moment a completely untrustworthy witness. In other words, the further I got in my very slight excursion into occult experiment, the further I was from intelligence, veracity, and honesty. The definite result of these experiments for me was a conviction that, at any rate, no man's word about automatic writing is worth the breath that utters it. The thing is not all fraud—there is something very queer about it ; but not the least phase of the queerness is that it is constantly, increasingly credulous, tricky, and mendacious.

In reflecting on these three experiences, I found them by and by grouping themselves as three stages of what I may call a specific mental or moral disorder. The first and simplest was the automatic writing whose ill effects induced me to abandon the whole thing. The second was the mediumistic trance, in which a woman whom I believe honest in her natural character hypnotized herself, and in the hypnotic state became perhaps abnormally perspicacious, and almost certainly a dangerous charlatan. The third was the elaborately dishonest mummery of materialization, where the fraud was so palpable that it seemed almost indubitably deliberate from beginning to end. But comparing this deliberate fraud with the simpler phases of occultism that I had observed, I found myself more and more disposed to believe it a kind of deliberate fraud, in all respects debasing, into which I could easily conceive an originally honest person to be unwittingly led.

III

ALL this time my impressions of Salem witchcraft had been derived from two absorbing days that I had passed with Mr. Upham's book some years ago. It had never occurred to me to question his conclusions ; nor would it have occurred to me had I not been called on to make a careful study of the life and character of Cotton Mather,

whom I found on intimate acquaintance by no
means the deliberate villain I had been led to believe him. In making that study, I had occasion
to read the original evidence in the witch-trials.*
And what most impressed me in that evidence
was its startling familiarity. The surroundings
were in all respects different from anything I
had known. In a century and a society far more
remote from us in condition than they are in
time, certain unhappy people were bringing
against others more unhappy still charges that
involved their lives. But the controlling spirit,
the atmosphere of this grotesque tragedy was
something I had known in the flesh. Whoever
has frequented materialization *séances*, and who
then reads with sympathetic imagination the
broken records of the witch-trials, can hardly
help admitting, I think, that these things are of
the same kind. There is fraud in both—terribly
tragic fraud then, grotesquely comic fraud now—
but in both the fraud is of the same horrible
vapourous kind ; and in both there is room for
a growing doubt whether there be not in all this
more than fraud and worse. If there be, that
mysterious thing is subtly evil beyond words ; if
there be an incarnate spirit of evil, then that mysterious thing is the direct work of that spirit.

* Woodward, W. E. Records of Salem Witchcraft,
1691–92, copied from the original documents. Roxbury,
1864–65, 2 vols , 4to. (Woodward's Hist. Ser., vols. 1, 2.)

The Nineteenth Century has discarded the Devil; to the Seventeenth Century, at least in New England, he was just as real as God. And the sin that transcended all other sin that could be done by the fallen children of Adam was the sin of those who, despairing of Heaven, leagued themselves before their time with Hell.

This is not the moment to analyze in detail the tremendous force of that doctrine of election which underlies Calvinism—the creed that for seventy years dominated New England. But whoever would understand the society from whose midst sprang the witches and the witch-judges of 1692 must never forget the grim creed which, declaring that no man could be saved but by the special grace of God, and that the only test of salvation was ability to exert the will in accordance with His, bred in the devout, and in whoever was affected by their counsels, an habitual introspection, and an habitual straining for mystical intercourse with the spiritual world, to-day almost inconceivable. In a world dominated by a creed at once so despairing and so mystic, it would not have been strange if now and then wretched men, finding in their endless introspection no sign of the divine marks of grace, and stimulated in their mysticism beyond modern conception by the churches that claimed and imposed an authority almost unsurpassed in history, had been tempted to seek, in premature

alliance with the powers of evil, at least some
semblance of the freedom that their inexorable
God had denied them. It was such an alliance
with which the Salem witches were charged. It
is just such miserable debasement of humanity as
should follow such an alliance that pervades the
evidence of the witch-trials, just as to-day it
pervades the purlieus of those who give themselves up to occultism in its lower forms.

IV

THE question I asked myself, when this view
of the matter became clear to me, was whether in
this evidence I could find traces of the other
stages of occultism to which I have already called
your attention. To answer this question to anybody's satisfaction would need longer and more
careful study than I have been able to give the
documents; but what little study I have had
time for has suggested to me, more and more
strongly, that prolonged study might yield surprising results. I will try very briefly to analyze
the evidence, to show what I mean.

It is not generally remembered, in spite of
Mr. Upham's admirable work, that the great bulk
of this evidence is what was called spectral. A
girl, for example, was bewitched, and testified
that the physical torture she was apparently
undergoing was caused by the conduct of the

apparition of one of the accused—an apparition providentially invisible to whoever was not bewitched. It was the acceptance by the court of this obviously worthless evidence that hanged the witches; it was the throwing out of such evidence that brought the witch-trials to a close. It was his momentary faith in such evidence—not in the horrible reality of witchcraft itself—that Samuel Sewall publicly repented in the Old South Church. And in analyzing the records of these old trials, we must put aside, once for all, every particle of spectral evidence, except as it tells against the witnesses themselves.

In a way, however, spectral evidence tells against the witnesses themselves rather startlingly. It was often accompanied in full court, by conduct that went far to make judges and attendants believe it. I cite almost at random, a single example of what I mean. In the examination of Rebecca Nurse is this passage :*

"Why should not you also be guilty for your apparition doth hurt also.

"Would you have me bely myself.

"*She held her neck on one side, and accordingly so were the afflicted taken.*"

A moment later—"Nurse held her neck on one side and Eliz. Hubbard (one of the sufferers) had her neck set in that posture whereupon another patient Abigail Williams, cryed out, set up Goody Nurse's head, the maid's neck will be broke, and when some set up Nurse's head Aa-

*1: 86, 87.

ron Wey, observed yᵗ Betty Hubbards was immediately righted."

This tells nothing whatever against Rebecca Nurse. What it tells against Betty Hubbard would have seemed a few years ago merely that she was a deliberate and unprincipled trickster. To-day, I think, it goes far to suggest a much less simple state of things ; namely, that Betty Hubbard was a hypnotic subject, so far gone as to be instantly affected by the slightest suggestion from a person on whom her diseased attention was concentrated. And it is typical of things that occurred throughout the sessions of the witch-courts. I am no expert in hypnotism, but what little I have read and seen of it so exactly corresponds with so much that is in this witch-evidence that I should be gravely surprised if experts who examined the evidence did not find the evidence going far to suggest that almost all the bewitched were probably victims of hypnotic excesses.

It is only in recent times, I believe, that careful study of the still mysterious and dangerous phenomena of hypnotism has tended to show that it depends far more on the subject than on the operator, and that a good subject, by careful concentration of attention, can hypnotize himself. That the bewitched sufferers at Salem often hypnotized themselves is highly probable. Here is another extract from the evidence—this time

from one of those unaccountable confessions which
have so baffled cool critics.*

"Now Mary Warren fell into a fit, and some of the
afflicted cryed out that she was going to confess, but Goody
Korey and Procter and his wife came in their apparition
and struck her down and said she should tell nothing.

"Mary Warren continued a good space in a fit, that she
did neither see, nor hear, nor speak.

"Afterward she started up, and said I will speak and
cryed out, Oh ! I am sorry for it, I am sorry for it, and
wringed her hands and fell a little while into a fit again
and then came to speak, but immediately her teeth were
set, and then she fell into a violent fit and cryed out, Oh
Lord help me ! Oh Good Lord save me !

"And then afterward cryed again, I will tell, I will tell
and then fell into a dead fit again "— which continued
until " she was ordered to be had out."

A little later she was "called in afterward in private
before magistrates and ministers.

"She said I shall not speak a word ; but I will I will
speak Satan.—She saith she will kill me. Oh ! she says
she owes me a spite and will claw me off.

"Avoid Satan, for the name of God Avoid and then fell
into fits again ; and cryed will ye, I will prevent ye in the
name of God."—

But in spite of her will, her fits persisted and " her lips
were bit so that she could not speak so she was sent away."

Within two days she made an elaborate, and
apparently mendacious confession of all sorts of
occult absurdity, beginning with the assertion
that her master and mistress had forced her into

* 1 : 120.

witchcraft, making her sign a book, and that they had made her stick a pin into a puppet, and so on.

Though not disposed to put much credence in this testimony against her employers, I am nevertheless very much struck by the likeness between this poor creature's conduct before the Salem magistrates and ministers, and the conduct of the trance-medium in Boston, who, as she was emerging at my request from her trance, begged me to save her from the horrible spectre she thought she saw in the corner. This medium was undoubtedly given to hypnotizing herself. How she had learned to do so I do not know. Is there not reason to guess that Mary Warren may have been given to hypnotizing herself, too ; and that very possibly she may have been taught to do so ?

In the midst of all this horrible confusion, then, there are glimpses of two of the stages of occultism to which I bore personal testimony. Is there any of the third, such as I dabbled in myself? Of automatic writing, I have found no trace ; that experiment I conceive to be a very modern one. But here is what poor Giles Corey testified against his wife : *

" Last Satturday in the Evening Sitting by the fire my wife asked me to go to bed. I told her I would go to prayer and when I went to prayer I could not utter my desires w^h any sense, *not open my mouth to speake*,† my wife did perceive itt and came toward me and said she

* 1 : 55–56.   † These italics are mine.

was coming to me.   After this in a little space I did according TO MY MEASURE attend the duty . . . My
wife hath ben wont to sett up after I went to bed and I
have perceived her to kneel doun on the harth as if she
were at prayer but heard nothing."

A mere question of temper, if you please ; but
if he had set about to describe an elementary hypnotic experiment, could he have said much otherwise ?   And is that kneeling figure at the hearth,
in the flickering firelight of two centuries ago,
quite godly in aspect ?
     Again : *

"John Blye Senior agett about 57 yeers and William
Blye aged about 15 years both of Salem Testifieth and
sayth yt being Imployed by Bridgitt Boshop Alies Oliuer
of Salem to helpe take doune ye Cellar wall of The Owld
house she formerly Lived in wee ye sd Deponents in holes
in ye sd owld wall belonging to ye sd Cellar found seuerall
popitts made up of Raggs And hoggs Brussells wth head-
les pins in Them.   wth ye points outward and this was
about Seaven years Last past."

Children's toys, to a nineteenth-century mind.
But all through the records of mediæval witchcraft and magic lie just such children's toys which
the world believed very fatal engines of death.   I
spoke of that testimony the other day to a friend
who happens to be—what I am far from being—
an ardent believer in that prevalent mysticism
called Christian Science.   To me, I said, the evi-

*1 : 163.

6

dence went a good way to show that somebody
had actually been trying in Salem to see whether
by sticking pins into a doll you could not torture
the enemy that the doll represented; the practice
certainly had existed in Europe, absurd as it must
seem to us.   To my surprise, my friend replied
that to her it did not seem absurd at all ; any believer in Christian Science, she went on, knew
that by concentrating your mind on an absent
person you could affect that person for good or
for ill; and that while the actual sticking of pins
into dolls could never directly hurt anything but
the dolls, it could help a malevolent mind so to
concentrate itself on the person a doll represented
as to injure him with far less effort than when
there was no doll to aid it; which view, she
added, was the view of Paracelsus.

I mention that case just to remind you how
curiously some of the educated minds of our
own time are recurring to kinds of mysticism
that have so long seemed purely superstitious;
how much more credible witchcraft is than it
used to be, now that we see these honest, intelli-
gent mystics all about us.

For only change the impulse of these very
people from the pure one it generally is, to the
base one that was held to actuate the witches,
and you have at your very firesides not a few examples of what witches were.   And do not the
silenced husband of Martha Corey, and the pin-

riddled dolls hidden in Bridget Bishop's cellar
wall go at least a little way to suggest that perhaps they had made unholy experiments?

Only a little way, I hasten to add. No one can
be better aware than I that such evidence as I have
offered here is very slight—at best not more than
suggestive. Nor can anyone know better than I
what I cannot too earnestly repeat, that I have
neither the scientific nor the historical learning necessary to make anything I should say
more than suggestive to better and wiser students. But this evidence, typical of much more
that can be dug out of those bewildering old
documents, will show you the sort of thing
that has led me both to believe that there was
abroad in 1692 an evil quite as dangerous as any
still recognized crime, and to wonder whether
some of the witches, in spite of the weakness and
falsity of the evidence that hanged them, may not
after all have deserved their hanging.

V

It remains for me to show why I believe this
evil so serious and the crime of whoever com-
mitted it in the seventeenth century so gross. I
cannot do so better than by repeating some words
I published a few months ago : *

If, as modern science tends to show, human

* In my Life of Cotton Mather, pp. 95-96.

beings are the result of a process of evolution from lower forms of life, there must have been in our ancestral history a period when the intelligence of our progenitors was as different from the modern human mind as were their remote aquatic bodies from the human form we know to-day. It seems wholly conceivable, then, that in the remote psychologic past of our race there may have been in our ancestors certain powers of perception which countless centuries of disuse have made so rudimentary that in our normal condition we are not conscious of them. But if such there were, it would not be strange that, in abnormal states, the rudimentary vestiges of these disused powers of perception should sometimes be revived. If this were the case, we might naturally expect two phenomena to accompany such a revival: in the first place, as such powers of perception belong normally to a period in the development of our race when human society and moral law have not yet appeared, we should expect them to be intimately connected with a state of emotion that ignores the moral sense, and so to be accompanied by various forms of misconduct; in the second place, as our chief modern means of communication — articulate language — belongs to a period when human intelligence has assumed its present form, we should expect to find it inadequate for the expression of facts which it never professed to cover, and so

we should expect such phenomena as we are considering to be accompanied by an erratic, impotent inaccuracy of statement, which would soon
shade into something indistinguishable from deliberate falsehood. In other words, such phenomena would naturally involve, in whoever abandons
himself to them, a mental and moral degeneracy
which anyone who believes in a personal devil
would not hesitate to ascribe to the direct inter-
vention of Satan.

Now what disposes me, scientifically a layman
I cannot too earnestly repeat, to put faith in this
speculation concerning occultism is that mental
and moral degeneracy—credulity and fraud—seem
almost invariably so to entangle themselves with
occult phenomena that many cool-headed persons
are disposed to assert the whole thing a lie. To
me it does not seem so simple. I incline more
and more to think that necromancers, witches,
mediums—call them what you will—actually do
perceive in the infinite realities about us things
imperceptible to normal human beings ; but that
they perceive them only at a sacrifice of their
higher faculties—mental and moral—not inaptly
symbolized in the old tales of those who sell
their souls.

If this be true, such an epidemic of witchcraft
as came to New England in 1692 is as diabolical
a fact as human beings can know ; unchecked, it
can really work mischief unspeakable. For un-

checked it would mean that more and more human beings would give themselves up to deliberate, or perhaps instinctive, effort to retrace the steps by which human intelligence, in countless centuries, has slowly risen from the primitive consciousness of the brute creation.

VI

To my mind, then, the fatally tragic phase of the witch trials is not that there was no evil to condemn, but that the unhappy victims of the trials were condemned literally on clairvoyant evidence. And what I have already said shows that in all probability those really guilty of the nameless crime I have tried to indicate were, in my opinion, not so often the witches as the bewitched.

But let us look at the matter a little more closely again. These wretched bewitched girls were in all probability victims of hypnotic excess. In all probability they had learned, willingly or unwillingly, to hypnotize themselves. Is there not a likelihood, then, that first of all they may have been hypnotized by others? And is there not, in the records of those terrible days, some faint suggestion that among those who first dragged the wretched girls down may have been some of the accused? The actual charges are sometimes manifestly false, almost always utterly incredible—lying, contradictory, vapourous—but beneath them all there remains a something which would make me guess that not all of the accused believed themselves innocent.

Put yourself for a moment in the place of those petty New England Calvinists, born and bred under an iron creed that forbade all hope of salvation to any but the elect of a capricious God. Fancy yourself toiling for years in vain to make your human will agree with His, to find in yourself the divine marks of grace. Then fancy yourself, in a moment of despair, toying with occult experiment—not as a scientific observer of the Nineteenth Century, but as a creed-ridden zealot of the Seventeenth, bound to believe that mysterious phenomena are the direct handiwork of either God or Satan. Fancy yourself finding that you could exercise over other and weaker wills than yours, that power which, under the name of hypnotism, scientific folks are studying to-day, and not a few of them denouncing as terribly dangerous. Fancy yourself finding that the more you exercised this power the more your victims yielded to it. Remember the debasement and the fraud that come as hardly resistible temptations to dabblers in occultism to-day. And then ask yourselves if anyone who yielded himself up in old Salem to such temptations as these, could have doubted that, in the Devil's mysterious way, he was doing the Devil's chosen work.

I cannot assert a single one of the dead witches

to have been such a figure as I have asked you to
fancy. But I can assert that if any of them were
by chance such a figure—and it seems to me
that careful study might go far to show that more
than one of them may have been—then the
dreadful fate that came to him, though it came
through evidence hopelessly weak and false, was
his moral due.

VII

I HAVE said enough to suggest to you the view
of Salem witchcraft that has forced itself on me.
From personal observation I have seen enough of
modern occultism, of the lower kind, to believe
it unholy. From the evidence of the witch-trials
I have gathered hints enough to make me believe
that beneath its horrible vapourous confusion lurks
just such unholiness as I have seen in the flesh.
And no one who knows a bit of the inner history
of New England Puritanism can doubt that if this
be true, then there were in old Salem men and
women who had deliberately sinned against God.
I have told all this in a manner that may well
have seemed too personal, too assertive of myself.
I have chosen to tell it thus deliberately. No
one can be better aware than I that, to be proved,
such views as I have suggested need the full
authority that should come from years of scientific
and of historical research. No one can know
better than I how far I am from such learning as

should give my words authority. But sometimes, I think, a frank statement of how an old matter looks to a fresh eye that glances at it never so superficially, may suggest to eyes familiar with it, views that their very familiarity would have prevented them from seeing for themselves. Such a service as this is among the best that men of letters can do for men of learning. And it is only as one who has tried to make himself a man of letters that I have earned the privilege of telling here not what is known of old Salem, but what seems to me perhaps knowable.

One reflection I shall venture to add. It is customary to regard the witch-trials as historically unimportant, except as a dreadful example of human delusion. If the views presented in this paper are valid, however, the witch-trials, far from being fruitless, may have accomplished a result of lasting importance in the history of New England. There was little more playing with occultism here, I think, until modern spiritualism arose, to be followed by the excessive interest in occult matters so notable within the last ten years. It seems more than possible, then, that the witch-trials, surrounding the whole subject with horror, may actually have checked for more than a century the growth of a tendency which unchecked, in the formative period of our national life, might gravely have demoralized our national character.

V

AMERICAN LITERATURE

[An Address made at Vassar College, on January 27, 1893.]

AMERICAN LITERATURE

I

Among the Christmas-cards that lately filled the windows of Cambridge shops was one that clearly distinguished itself from the rest. Quite large enough to frame, it included six oval *passe-partouts;* and from these, executed with conventional flattery, gazed six heroic faces : the faces of Emerson, Longfellow, Lowell, Whittier, Hawthorne, and Dr. Holmes. In the midst of chromolithographed angels, stars of Bethlehem, belfries, snow-storms, grotesques, these six worthies of New England were pleasant things to look at. In the midst of mere conventions any fact not yet lifelessly conventional is a pleasant thing, and surely an American can hardly look at those six faces without a feeling of pride. Here are men of our own blood and almost of our own time, men whom any of us that has reached the threshold of middle age might have known well. Only one of them is with us still, but the others are gone only a little before. We shall all pass together into that shadowy future where the generations shall merge. In a sense, then, these men are our leaders; and they are noble leaders to follow. Whatever their shortcomings, whatever their errors, the world rarely affords the spectacle of such a group : silently chosen from among their fellows for honest work honestly done, honest words honestly spoken, these men, as we study their lives, triumphantly prove how nearly stainless human manhood may be.

In certain moods, one goes on to say, this is answer enough for whoever still questions the claim of American literature to a place among the literatures of the ages. In such moods one has only to look at these faces, to utter these names. The questioner whom these will not silence, one feels, is a questioner who will never accept an answer. We know the lives of these men ; and no lives were ever better. We know their work, which any man may look at. That is enough. Let us trust posterity.

Posterity will judge ; that is certain. It will judge, too, with unthinking impartiality—without acrimony, without tenderness. What mankind wants or needs it will preserve and remember ; what mankind finds useless it will cast aside and forget. That is what makes the past seem heroic to all eyes not unduly sharpened by the engines of science. "It is the sin and the tumult and the passion of human life that die. Enshrined in art the beauty of the old days lives, and it will live forever." And even though science nowadays teach us the suggestive truth that the old days which we have reverenced were after all, when the sun still shone on them, days of turbulence and wickedness disheartening as any that surges about us now, that same science, one often thinks, is prone to forget the deep law of human nature which makes each generation, in the end, remember instinctively of those that are gone before only or chiefly those traits and deeds which shall add to the wisdom and the power of humanity.

So from among the written records of past time the posterity of which you and I are part has unwittingly selected some which are of lasting value. These we call literature. What literature contains for us already, nobody quite knows as yet. Modern learning, they say, at last exploring the mysteries of the East, discerns and reveals to us more and more records, unknown to us for centuries amid what used to seem the outer darkness of India or China, from which perhaps we of the Western world may by and by glean things worth having. But our own possessions are already rich. We have the great literature of the Hebrews; we have the literatures of Greece and Rome, the literatures of Italy and Spain, and France, and Germany, and England. It is to this list that we so confidently try to add our own literature of America.

Already, our confidence seems less certain than

when we were considering by themselves the six worthies of New England. Already we begin to see that, discarding all literatures but those of Europe, there is a group of great figures among whom Homer and Dante and Shakespeare are perhaps supreme, but only in a great company of notable personages pressing closely about them. It is in such company as this that we claim place for Emerson, and Longfellow, and Lowell, and Whittier, and Hawthorne, and Holmes. Very clearly, we cannot claim it as confidently as when at first we only looked at their faces and remembered their lives. To be confident at all, in fact, one way or the other, we must hesitate. We must ask ourselves first what literature is; then by what right any men or any people may claim a place in its history or its hierarchy; and finally, what these heroes of ours and our other fellow-countrymen have done to make good the claim that we rather urge for them than they for themselves.

II

LITERATURE, then, we may perhaps define as the lasting expression in words of the meaning of life.

Whatever our philosophy, we must admit that to every conscious being life presents itself as an endlessly interwoven web of impressions to which we give the names thought and emotion.

What things are in themselves no philosophy has
finally settled; but how things present themselves to human intelligence even the vulgar instinctively know, each for himself. This instinctive knowledge, this fundamental sense of the
reality of thought and emotion which each of us
possesses, which all of us share in common, grows,
as we contemplate it, more and more wonderful.
Our senses bring to our intelligence images of
material things,—commonplace, beautiful, repel-
lent. Some faculty within us brings to our intelligence conceptions of pleasure and of pain, of
utility and of danger, of good and of evil. To
each of us, even before he is grown old enough
to talk, this great panorama of human experience
is a thing that has already begun to impress him
somehow. In what seems inextricable confusion,
he is aware of something not himself that defines
itself in a thousand phantasmagoric forms, endlessly awakening in him those myriad reactions
that together make the individuality by which he
is known to others. These impressions and these
reactions slowly group themselves. By and by
one comes to know some of them as hateful, some
as noble, some as alluring. By and by one grows
to feel that some of these should be sought, some
repelled. High or low, good or evil, spiritual
or material, ideals declare themselves. At most
times we are merely aware of this vast web of experience weaving itself inexorably about our in-

7

telligence from without and from within. When, at rare moments, we pause to contemplate it, we generally contemplate it only in fragments. There are other moments, far more rare, when for awhile we try to contemplate it as a whole. When thus, deliberately or instinctively, we pause to contemplate life, in whole or in its smallest part, we are sure to discover that what we contemplate impresses us in a way peculiar to itself and to us. In other words, it has a meaning, be that meaning only a transient sense of vulgar pleasure or pain, or be it what we deem the nobler conceptions of philosophy or religion. And this meaning, which we have power to express, is the substance of which all art, and so all literature, is made.

We have power to express it, to share it with others. This power we are always exerting—in every word we utter, in every quiver of muscle that tells the unending story of human pleasure and pain, grief and joy. Most of our expressions, incalculably most, are trivial things and passing, little more significant than the purrs or the whines of animals that we are fond of calling lower than ourselves. Sometimes, however, instinctively or deliberately, men express the meaning of life in a way that is not quite trivial or passing. In plastic form, from the scratched bones of prehistoric caverns to the splendour of Periclean Athens or the Italy of the Medici, there have been records of what human eyes have seen that make humanity permanently richer. In music, from the twanging bowstring of savages to the æthereal orchestra of Beethoven or of Wagner, there have been such records of what human ears have heard. This protean meaning of life has phases that are lasting, the record of which, by whoever is fortunate enough or great enough to perceive them, is permanently significant. Such records, such expressions as these are what make each generation richer in the possession of more and more experiences which the inexorable conditions of space and of time have forbidden them in the flesh. Sometimes these records have a significance chiefly sympathetic, declaring through the centuries how men have been men from oldest time. Sometimes they actually reveal to us aspects of life which otherwise we might never have known. Sympathetic or enriching, these records which are permanently significant, these expressions of the meaning of life which are lasting, are the body of all art, and so of all literature.

Of these lasting expressions of the meaning of life, some, as we have seen, are in plastic form, bearing their message, in architecture, in sculpture, in painting, to whoever having eyes will see; some, in the form of music, bear their message to whoever having ears will hear. Some, however, and these perhaps the most definitely significant, phrase themselves not in these forms, which the laws of human nature render in each generation practicable only by the few who are born with the power of mastering them; but in that other form, not more easy of mastery though so incalculably more familiar in practice, by which human beings are agreed to conduct the affairs of daily life. It is such lasting expressions of the meaning of life as these—such lasting expressions as are phrased in words—to which we give the name literature.

III

By what right, was our second question, may any man or any people claim a serious place in the history of literature or in its hierarchy? Before we try to answer this with certainty, I think, we shall do well to consider perhaps the most notable feature of the vehicle which literature employs—the chief characteristic of words.

Lines and colours, the vehicles of the plastic arts, are essentially imitative; whoever has looked at nature can recognize in the work of architect, sculptor, or painter the effort to make its literal or conventional image. The very vagueness, the intangible æthereality of the emotions most fitly phrased by the melodies and the harmonies of music make these melodies and harmonies elusively, mysteriously intelligible to whoever has felt the experience that gave them birth. Words, however, though we use them so constantly that we hardly know ourselves in other than verbal terms, are neither imitative, like lines and colours, nor inevitable as the strains of music. Essentially their meaning is as arbitrary as that of the letters by which we have agreed to symbolize them. Instinctively fit as the words seem by which you and I exchange our thoughts, we all know that they are meaningless, except after months or years of study, to anyone whose native tongue is not English; and we have only to glance at any obvious monument of Roman antiquity—at the Arch of Constantine, for example—to feel the difference between the lastingly intelligible plastic form in which imperial power was expressed, and the puzzling obscurity of even the simplest inscription phrased in terms no longer used by human beings. Intelligible to those who are agreed to use them, these arbitrary symbols that we call words have no meaning to those who have not learned, by environment or by study, what meaning has been attached to them by the tacit consent of those by whom they are used. Arbitrary, intelligible only to those whom chance or effort has made masters of them, these words which literature employs to express the lasting meaning of life vary with every language that human beings have grown to use. According as we know language or not, then, literature is either the most familiar of arts or the most unmeaning.

This very diversity of languages, however, seriously as it must limit the range and the power of any single literature, greatly extends the range and the power of literature in its broader sense. No commonplace, when one considers, is much more pregnant than that which asserts the inevitable discrepancy between the number of ideas that form part of every man's experience and the number of words at his disposal to name them. It is a large dictionary that contains a hundred thousand words; and a copious author who uses of these above ten or twelve thousand. Yet the varying experiences even of a single conscious day might almost be numbered by millions. At best, the vocabulary of any language names only in a tentative, approximate way the thoughts and emotions it recognizes. At best, any grammar expresses the relations of these ideas within very narrow limits. In the hurried intercourse of every day we are too busy, our perceptions too much blunted by habit, to be aware of how little beyond the experiences common to every day the language at our disposal will express. But try for a moment to phrase any idea not quite familiar, try to impress even your most familiar idea on some one to whom it is strange, and you are face to face with the inevitable inadequacy of language to do more than faintly symbolize the immaterial reality of thought and emotion that you know within yourself. What is thus true of us as individuals is true of those races, as races, that have agreed to use a common tongue. Try to translate the simplest words from the languages most intimately connected with ours—*ennui*, for example, or *blasé*—and you will often find that though we know just what they mean we have no name of our own by which English-speaking folks have agreed to express it. Try to translate the title of Dante's "Convito": you will say *feast*, but *feast* combines for us no two words that mean by themselves *a living together*. These trite illustrations are enough. Each language names ideas in a way peculiarly its own. The common agreement on arbitrary symbols that at length results in the vocabulary of any language is sure to produce symbols that stand for peculiar aspects of the real thought and emotion which language tries to define—for aspects, in other words, which differ from those named by any other tongue. And what is thus plainly true of words by themselves is just as true of words in combination. The difficulty we find in mastering a foreign grammar is more than formal; each foreign grammar defines in ways of its own relations of thought which our grammar neglects, and neglects meanwhile relations that our grammar defines. What can express in English, for example, the relations so definitely expressed by the inflections of Latin or of Greek? What in Latin or Greek the almost sexual gender of English? In its vocabulary, in its grammar, in its entirety, each language must express the lasting meaning of life in aspects different from those expressed by any other. Limited as the range of any one language must be, then, or of any one literature, the range of language and literature, in their broadest sense, may be called almost limitless.

A growing sense of this perhaps underlies the impatience of some modern scholars with the old classification of literature. The notion of national literatures, they feel, is artificial, archaic. It were better to gather all literature together, to study it comparatively, neglecting the accident of phrase, looking rather at the growing, developing range of thought and emotion that the combined literatures of the ages express. In this feeling there is much that commands one's sympathy. Words as words are dead things—arbitrary symbols incredibly less meaning in themselves than the lines of plastic art or the strains of music. The pedantry that so enshrouds linguistic learning, too, even in its innermost strongholds, makes these dead words often seem farther from vitality than in fact they are. Yet no impatience with artificiality, with archaism, with pedantry, can conceal in the end the actual fact that underlies the old classification of national literatures. Each national literature expresses the lasting meaning of life in its own peculiar language; and each language, we have seen, names the innumerable phenomena of life in aspects and in combinations that to a greater degree or a less, every other language neglects. In the nature of language it seems inherently necessary that as each new tongue develops to a point where it can lastingly express the meaning of life it must express that meaning in a manner of its own.

We can answer our question better now. By what right, we asked, may any man or any people claim a serious place in the history of literature or in its hierarchy? In its history, we may say, by one of two rights : either by expressing in words some phase of the lasting meaning of life which words have not hitherto expressed ; or by expressing some known phase of that meaning in words more lasting than those which have hitherto expressed it. In the hierarchy of literature, we may go on to say, a serious place can be claimed only when both rights are combined—when a man or a people has given to the world an expression of the meaning of life at once new and final.

It is for expressing a strange, dreamy, fleeting poetry of feeling that people are tardily according a place in the history of literature to the vanished poetry of the British Celts. It is for a vague, half-slumbrous sense of Titanic awakening —God knows to what end—that many are to-day disposed to accord such a place to the new literature of Russia. It is for startling flashes of insight through the murky shams of modern con-

vention that of late it has been the fashion to
claim such a place for Henrik Ibsen, and chiefly
by right of his genius for the literature of Norway.   To pass to greater things, it is not for freshness of thought but for unsurpassed power of
condensation and epigram that we may most certainly claim such a place for the ultimately com-
pact literature of the Latin tongue.   It is for a
sense of order, of lucidity, of amenity unequalled
in any other modern language that so many accord the first place in contemporary literature to
the literature of France.

To pass to greater things still, the literature of
the Hebrews most of us know only in the modern
versions by which, since the time of Luther, it
has become the great motive force of the Protes-
tant world ; but as version after version adds each
something to our composite notion of what the
fact that all stand for must be, not a few of us are
willing to believe that in its native form that
literature, expressing spiritual truths as none has
expressed them since, may well be such as to give
colour to the old dreams of verbal inspiration.
The literature of Greece is half closed to men of
our time by the transitional pedantry that in our
school-days has passed for education ; yet even
we can appreciate it enough to know that in its
native form it expresses its meaning with an exquisitely modulated precision not to be dreamed
of by those who know it only in the guise of

translation; and those who know it only thus seem more and more aware that even to them it phrases, in a way that nothing can supplant, the view of life which has made so many thoughtful generations deem the word *classic* only less sacred than the word *holy*. So far, perhaps, I have spoken hearsay. There are two supreme writers —Dante and Shakespeare—whom it has been my own fortune to know from the very words they wrote. And as the years pass I realize for myself more and more—as all who know supreme things must realize—why such work as theirs were alone enough to give a lasting place in the hierarchy of literature to the languages in which each has finally expressed a meaning of life which before him none had quite perceived and after him none need phrase.

We have doubtless seemed to stray from our subject, from America. Yet with less general consideration we should hardly have been able to discuss American literature fairly. For in all fairness we are bound to admit that only by such rights as we have tried to define may any man or any people claim a serious place in the history of literature or in its hierarchy.

IV

THE question that is left us is becoming more definite. Have we Americans as a people, or have men among us as individuals made good any claim to a serious position in literature ? To put the question bluntly, What does American literature amount to ?

We should be able to see that the question is not easy to answer off-hand; that the fine, if over-sensitive patriotism which so often impels us to assert that our literature amounts to pretty much all creation, is little more reasonable than the still more sensitive reaction from such patriotism, which makes some of us occasionally feel like saying that it does not amount to anything. The question is really one of simple fact ; but of simple fact that is rather hard to get hold of. In all the other literatures we have touched on there is one important trait which ours obviously lacks. Celtic Britain, Russia, Norway, Rome, France, have had each a language of its own ; so have the Hebrews, and Greece, and Italy, and England. The one fact which we must definitely admit about ourselves is that for better or worse we think and speak in English. There are things called " Americanisms," of course, frequently discoverable only in dictionaries compiled elsewhere than in America. There is hardly one of the United States, however, whose current speech is so far removed from the normal standard of literary English as is the dialect of Devonshire or of Yorkshire. Whatever we have of our own, we have as yet no distinct language. When we ask if we have an American literature, then, we really mean to inquire whether as a people or as individuals we have added anything distinctively our own, in thought or in phrase, to that lasting expression in words of the meaning of life which is the common property of the English-speaking world.

V

In considering this question we may conveniently remind ourselves of the broad facts of our national history. The facts of national history are the memoranda of national experience. If in these we find experiences peculiarly ours, we shall have found at least the material for a national literature, whether we have used it or not.

Briefly, then, we may say that our national history covers about two hundred and fifty years; that, broadly speaking, it is the history of a series of emigrations from a highly civilized, overcrowded world,—in the beginning, to a wilderness where there was plenty of room, and until very lately to a continent, still unsettled in every sense of the word, where the material problems of life have presented themselves much less definitely than in Europe. Broadly speaking, the earlier of these emigrations were remarkable for excellence of personal quality; among the settlers of New England, for example, the proportion of people who amounted to something, cannot fail

to impress whoever studies the documents they
have left us. For nearly two centuries these emigrations were not remarkable either for excellence
of personal quality or for badness; they com-
prised good, every-day people whom any decent
community could absorb without danger. During the greater part of our own lifetimes the
quality of these emigrations has again become remarkable, until one may guess that not a few
native American hearts were tempted to greet
with un-Christian enthusiasm even the epidemic
cholera which lately checked, though only for a
little while, the influx of degradation that had
been swirling upon us from every moral and
political pest-hole in Europe and Asia. Broadly
speaking, the motive of the first emigration to
New England—the emigration whose traditions
have most profoundly affected our national
thought—was, in the words of Richard Mather, a
desire to remove

"from a place where all the ordinances of God cannot be
enjoyed unto a place where they may;"

in other words, the Puritan fathers were prepared
to make any sacrifice for the purpose—profoundly
human in spite of all their godliness—of managing their affairs, temporal and spiritual, in their
own way. Broadly speaking, the successive emigrants not personally noteworthy, who for two centuries or so added their energies to those of the
fathers and their direct descendants, came hither

for the purpose of making their fortunes. The unhappily remarkable emigration of the last generation seems to have been impelled by a purpose less definite than these; but it is not easy to discover for such unfortunate people as now swarm about us any much more useful function in human society than the making of mischief. Broadly speaking, then, the social aspect of our national history shows us first a people remarkable for self-assertion and singularly free from the problems which the struggle for life presents in any densely populous community; secondly, a people whom this very freedom permits to attain, with less concentrated effort than others, a remarkable degree of rather irresponsible material prosperity; and, finally, a people whose very prosperity has brought upon them, in their New World, almost precisely the problems which until lately they have prided themselves upon having escaped or solved.

Politically, our national history is even a more familiar commonplace. It begins with the development of communities geographically remote from the centre of power to a degree now inconceivable, and by this very fact both permitted and compelled to develop real centres of power within themselves. It proceeds through that great struggle . for national independence and unity in which all the mists of philanthropic and rhetorical bombast that now obscure it cannot conceal the victory of reality over sham, of facts over words and theories. It comprises that terrible experience of national distemper when within ourselves two systems that could not coexist fought, each nobly, to the death. It finds us now face to face with the world-old problem, new only to us among the nations, of how when the struggle for life grows fierce, human power can preserve those things which are good and repress those which are evil.

In our discussion of American literature, we may best put the present aside. And this for more reasons than one. Our present and our future, for one thing, differ little from the present and the future of all European humanity. If we face our problems differently, it is not because the problems themselves are different, but because our two or three centuries of American experience have made us other than we should have been had we remained with our kindred across the Atlantic. Again, no man can fitly estimate himself, nor can any period; it is as if a soldier or a captain, ignorant of his general's knowledge and plans, tried to tell in the midst of a campaign its whole history and significance. And less certainly, but more powerfully, a feeling perhaps sentimental but not fleeting, makes some of us dread to seek or to recognize in the actual world of which you and I are part actual signs of a great, lasting record of its meaning. For one

sometimes thinks that the history of fine art, in
all its phases, teaches a lesson that the lovers of
fine art dread to learn.   Such expressions of the
meaning of life as prove lasting, one feels in such
moods, are the final expressions of states of things
almost past.   In such moods, the stories of the
Athens of Pericles, of the Rome of Augustus
Cæsar, of the Italy of Raphael and of Michael
Angelo, of the England of Shakespeare, seem the
same; and these names seem to name only instances of an inexorable law.   The end of man,
one feels like saying, is expression; but expression is just as truly the end of man.   The songs
that live are the swan-songs.

Aspiration to make all our art fine — all our
records, of every kind, lasting and beautiful—is
surely a noble thing.   Not to foster, not to en-
courage such aspiration is just as surely ignoble.   But there are moods in which such aspiration seems something like earthly preparation for
heaven.   The best of us are really best because
they are constantly preparing themselves for
what inevitably must come.   When the time for
heavenly glory comes, of course, or for great artistic expression, it is only those who are best by the
noblest standards of human experience that are
anything like ready.   If on earth or in heaven,
then, we of America are ever to be lastingly noble,
we must never relax our effort always to be as
noble as we can; but the very end we hope for

8

is an end that at the same time we dread. As lovers of art we may well regret that among ourselves we find at this moment no expression of what this actual life of ours means which forces itself upon us as undoubtedly lasting. As patriots, though, and as human beings who love without knowing why this actual state of life that for a little while is ours, we may take comfort in the thought that our vital energies as a people are still thoughtlessly engaged in action, not yet thoughtfully or recklessly in contemplation or in expression. There are few surer warrants of the soundness of our national youth.

Our real meaning, then, when we ask what American literature amounts to, is this : Have we lasting expressions of the meaning of the past periods of American life, in words which have added either thought or phrase to the literature of the English language ?

VI

THE fathers of New England were almost as prolific in mind as in body. The fate of their intellectual offspring, too, resembled that of their physical — generally it did not survive. And tradition, remembering chiefly the titles of their sermons and their pamphlets and their treatises, much as it remembers the extremely Christian names of their children, reports their work as godly, narrow, dull, dreary, fruitless—anything, in short, that should repel a reader.

In a way, they have been unduly abused. People nowadays know so little of what Seventeenth-Century Yankees actually wrote, that it is perhaps worth our while to consider a bit of Seventeenth-Century Yankee narrative. It is from Cotton Mather's "Magnalia," where it closes his account of Theophilus Eaton, the first Governor of New Haven:

"His eldest son he maintained at the Colledge until he procceded master of arts; and he was indeed the son of his vows and *hopes*. But a severe catarrh diverted this young gentleman from the work of the ministry whereto his father had once devoted him; and a malignant fever then raging in those parts of the country, carried him off with his wife within two or three days of one another. This was counted the sorest of all the trials that ever befel his father in the 'days of the years of his pilgrimage;' but he bore it with a patience and composure of spirit which was truly admirable. His dying son looked earnestly on him, and said, 'Sir, what shall we do?' Whereto, with a well-ordered countenance, he replied, 'Look up to God!' And when he passed by his daughter, drowned in tears on this occasion, to her he said, 'Remember the sixth commandment: hurt not yourself with immoderate grief: remember Job, who said, "The Lord hath given, and the Lord hath taken away; blessed be the name of the Lord!" You may mark what a note the Spirit of God put upon it; "in all this Job sinned not, nor charged God foolishly:" God accounts it a charging of Him foolishly, when we don't submit unto His will patiently.' Accordingly, he now governed himself as one that had attained unto the rule of 'weeping as if we wept not;' for it being the Lord's day, he repaired unto the church in the *afternoon*, as he had been there in the *forenoon*, though he was never like to see his dearest son alive any more in this world. And though before the first prayer began, a messenger came to prevent Mr. Davenport's praying for the sick person, who was now *dead*, yet his affectionate father altered not his course, but *wrote* after the preacher as formerly; and when he came home he held on his former methods of divine worship in his family, not for the excuse of Aaron, omitting anything in the service of God. In like sort, when the people had been at the solemn interment of this his worthy son, he did with a very unpassionate aspect and carriage then say, 'Friends, I thank you all for your love and help, and for this testimony of respect unto me and mine: the Lord hath given, and the Lord hath taken: blessed be the name of the Lord!' Nevertheless, retiring hereupon into the chamber where his daughter then lay sick, some tears were observed falling from him while he uttered these words, 'There is a difference between a sullen silence or a stupid senseless-ness under the hand of God, and a child-like submission thereunto.'

"Thus continually he, for about a score of years, was the *glory* and *pillar* of New Haven colony. He would often say, 'Some count it a great matter to *die well*, but I am sure 'tis a great matter to *live well*. All our care should be while we have *life* to use it well, and so when death puts an end unto *that*, it will put an end unto all our cares.' But having excellently managed his care to *live well*, God would have him to *die well*, without any room or time then given him to take any *care* at all; for he enjoyed a death *sudden* to every one but himself! Having worshipped God with his family after his usual manner, and upon some occasion charged all the family to carry it well unto their mistress who was now confined by sickness, he supped, and then took a turn or two abroad for his meditations. After that he came in to bid his wife good-night, before he left her with her watchers; which when he did, she said, 'Methinks you look sad!' Whereto he replied, 'The differences risen in the church of Hartford make me so;' she then added, 'Let us even gó back to our native country again;' to which he answered, 'You may (and so she did), but I shall die here.' This was the last word that ever she heard him speak; for now retiring unto his lodging in another chamber, he was overheard about midnight fetching a *groan;* and unto one sent in presently to enquire how he did, he answered the enquiry with only saying, 'Very ill!' and without saying any more, he fell 'asleep in Jesus,' in the year 1657, loosing anchor from New Haven for the better."

A shorter extract could hardly give the full effect of this typical Puritan story. It is very foreign to our present ways of thought and speech. Perhaps it deserves all the epithets posterity unthinkingly gives it—godly, narrow, dull, dreary, what-not. Yet as one grows familiar with the literature for which it may fairly stand representative, one finds in it more and more not only a certain half-scriptural charm of style, but a genuinely interesting record of human experience. A strangely tense life it shows us, dull and trivial externally, commonplace in phrase, but in its essence intensely idealistic. This Theophilus Eaton is a man to whom the real things are the things unseen, to whom things seen are only passing shows. These passing shows, moreover, are of a very simple kind, because they were passing not in Cromwell's populous England but in a colony where, after all, nothing was yet actually more important than what went on of a Sunday at church. Cotton Mather, the writer of this story, lived two generations later; his life, in fact, was spent in fruitless efforts to maintain the principles that his "Magnalia" records—chief among which was the political supremacy of the clergy, which in Eaton's time had seemed assured. Cotton Mather lived so late that in his prime he sent a letter to the *Spectator*, or at least planned to send one, for there is no record of its reception. When he wrote this life of Eaton, Dryden's work was almost finished.

This contrast is what most impresses one, in the literary aspect of his narrative. The style has dignity, character, a fine rhythm of its own; no other could tell quite so well the story of what emigrant Puritanism meant. But in England such a style was obsolete. The "Magnalia" was published in the Eighteenth Century; body and soul it is a book of the Seventeenth. That sentence tells the whole story. Remote from the great world, the American colonies preserved, in somewhat fading colours, traditions that England had outgrown. We cannot assert that either in thought or in phrase they actually added to the literature of our language anything which that literature did not already possess.

VII

FOR Puritanism, which is all that the earlier literature of America voices, had exponents enough and to spare in England itself. The course of Puritanism in America, however, differed from its course in the mother country. There, its dominant power was short. The system of Calvin, to be sure, states the problems of life with a fidelity that to-day surprises any stranger who has known the system only by distorted tradition, or by verbal dogmas which time has stripped of their vital meaning even for those who utter them. Beneath it lies a profound, lasting sense of the actual evils which life, by inexorable law, is bound to develop in any dense population. What Calvinism regarded as evidence of the total depravity of man, indeed, is very like what modern science calls the struggle for existence. What it regarded as evidence for the doctrine of election is very like what people have in mind nowadays when they talk about the survival of the fittest. Such a struggle for such survival involves a good many problems, material and spiritual. These Calvinism states admirably; but it is one thing to state problems and another to solve them. The solution which Calvinism offers is not one, apparently, which—true or false—any dense, active population can be induced, for any length of time, to accept. In

England the facts on which the dogmas of Puritanism were based remained ; and the solution which Puritanism offered broke down. In America, almost to our own time, the facts have been greatly relaxed ; and the Calvinistic solution remained for generations as a dogmatic system, nominally dominant, but really losing itself more and more in such intricacies of logical abstraction as men will generally weave for themselves when stern fact does not check them.

While the forgotten theologians of our first century were thus making the logic whose ultimate monument is the "One-Hoss Shay," the social and political facts of American history, as we have seen, were pretty steadily developing themselves in the direction of an ideal whose name still remains, perhaps, the most instinctively inspiring to American ears—the ideal of independence. Socially, men were discovering that, if they neglected the theoretical principles of the fathers, and adhered only to the practical principle of insisting upon managing their affairs in their own way, they could so manage their affairs as to make themselves in the end a good deal better off than they were in the beginning. They were really started on that road to fortune-making which in our own time they have travelled so far as gravely to disturb some of our contemporaries who lag behind in the race. Politically, at the same time, they were discovering that small, homogeneous communities can really manage their public business much better than anybody else can manage it for them; and what is more, that whether they can or not, there was at that period no choice. Whence, by and by, common sense began apparently to confirm sundry vague notions of the divine rights of liberty and equality which the experience of our heterogeneous and overgrown communities makes some people at present think less axiomatic than of old. Meanwhile, it was evident to whoever calmly observed American human nature under these conditions, that while by no means celestial in perfection, it very generally developed traits which did not seem necessarily damnable. Theology, in fact, originally based on actual experience, was insensibly separating itself from experience; and experience was reaching fresh, unformulated conclusions of its own.

Hastily as we have considered these lines of thought, we have perhaps seen enough to account for the two Americans of the Eighteenth Century whose names most certainly survive in the history of American literature,—the two whose thought was most surely earnest enough, and whose phrase apt enough, to be read still. These are Jonathan Edwards and Benjamin Franklin. In the passionate effort of Edwards to revive the pristine force of orthodox Calvinism, the theology of the fathers reached the highest point. It was sincere, it was terribly earnest, it was almost impregnably logical; but it was so highly developed that even though we knew nothing of its circumstances we might shrewdly guess it to be, like so many great works of art, essentially a thing of the past. In point of fact, we know its circumstances. What it thought the innate depravity of human nature had so flourished along with it that Edwards preached and wrote to a world where year by year there were more and more men who felt in their bones that after all this was not so. In that very world, too, the cool common-sense that has made on the whole inefficient the later efforts of Calvinistic logic was voiced by " Poor Richard," and by that sturdy practical life of Franklin's whose self-written record remains among the best narratives of personal experience in the English language.

In the English language, we must remember,— the English language that is ours. Edwards and Franklin are surely figures that we may call our own. Almost as surely, though, they are figures that English literature may equally claim. In both thought and phrase they may have added a little to what English literature already possessed. It would be overbold, however, confidently to assert that either added anything more significant than an indication of how English human nature develops itself in a world where there is still room enough for every man to move freely.

VIII

FRANKLIN, however, is far more than a merely literary figure. It is the tradition of his life that has survived rather than any wide knowledge of what he wrote. No figure in our history is more generally remembered, nor any more deservedly ; for whatever his merits on a moral scale, the man was in his life first, last, and always an American. Shrewd common-sense never had a more palpable incarnation ; nor that peculiar, ever-present, not needlessly obtrusive personal independence which so generally makes a native Yankee, wherever he goes, a troublesome match for people who assume to be his betters. Himself, then, we remember first ; and if we are suddenly asked what he was besides being himself, our impulse would be in conveniently general terms to answer that he was a statesman and a philosopher.

In this double character, more than in anything he actually said or wrote, Franklin typifies something beyond the rational spirit of his own time, which put an end in America to the dominance of theological logic. From that time to ours the most serious expressions of American thought have been either political or philosophic. Before we consider, then, those later phases of American literature whose purpose is more purely artistic, we may conveniently remind ourselves first of the political literature, then of the philosophic, and finally of the peculiar fusion of the two that precede and surround them.

IX

FROM the middle of the Eighteenth Century to a time that we ourselves can remember, American public men produced a pretty steady flow of oratory. The standard speakers that, very possibly, are still among the most thumbed text-books of secondary schools, have made a good deal of this eloquence household words. From Patrick Henry and Otis to Daniel Webster and the dozens of lesser men who surrounded him, we are familiar with endless declamations which voice with varying merit the patriotic enthusiasm and vagaries of American independence. Much of this, at least to us of America, seems really fine and stirring; much of it, at least to some of us, is beginning to seem rather sonorous than significant. Ultimately true, though, or ultimately empty, it certainly phrases, with spontaneous enthusiasm, the thoughts and emotions which at critical moments have been the vital forces of our national history; and these thoughts and emotions, when we consider them coolly, appear to be just such as we should expect to arise among the conditions of life that we have considered. The dominant ideals that run through all this eloquence are the ideals of law and of right. These are not very clearly distinguished. In general, there seems to be an underlying feeling that if by any chance they are not identical they ought to be, and therefore will be. Anyhow, we ought all to be law-abiding, and all to be moral, and all to be at liberty to think and to behave as we choose within the obvious limits of law and morals. And what we ought to be we mean to be ; and that is American. So, being Americans, we are, generally speaking, pretty much what we ought to be. Incidentally, then, we are always in the right ; and whoever disagrees with us is consequently and obviously wrong, and ought to be made to understand it.

In this summary of the ultimate impression produced by the patriotic eloquence of our country there is perhaps a suggestion of caricature ; for the summary certainly neglects the most admirable emotional trait of the eloquence in question, —the sincerity, the enthusiasm, the tremendous motive power of such convictions as it phrases. In less critical moods one finds this enthusiasm heroically contagious ; this eloquence really seems to voice the meaning of life. If we ask ourselves, however, what phase of the meaning of life it lastingly voices our answer seems inevitable : very clearly it is a phase of human experience where for a while the troublesome pressure of external fact is blessedly relaxed.

In a society so simple as ours used to be, one man is really about as good as another. The experience of the generations that preceded the American Revolution, one may almost say of the generations that preceded the American Civil War, had confirmed those inspiring doctrines of human equality and fraternity which in reality we learned rather from the philosophical vagaries of Eighteenth-Century France than from the practical experience we inherit from law-abiding England. Our actual conduct was generally based on the sound old English traditions ; our words and our thoughts were, more than we have generally realized, borrowed from the cloud-spun theories of clever Frenchmen. We have never yet dreamed that our conduct and our speech do not agree ; and at the period we are now considering—the period that gave rise to the great century of American oratory—the theories that our oratory uttered actually came far nearer to correspondence with fact than is commonly the case in human history. Society was not yet complex enough to group itself in distinct, hostile classes. The only men who were really dangerous were the men who were not law-abiding or not good.

Here, then, one feels like saying, is at least one body of literature, whatever its final value, that is historically American. In a way it is. But turn to those very standard speakers in which we are most familiar with it. You will find there a great many examples of English oratory, too. Compare the speeches made in Parliament with the speeches made in Congress. You will find a difference, of course; but as you read on, you can hardly escape a growing doubt as to whether this difference is essential, a difference of kind. If you were lately vexed by a perhaps unsympathetic summary of American eloquence, you may be consoled by observing how much of it might be applied to British eloquence, too. Less hampered by the pressure of material facts, less restrained by the presence of keen critics, our orators perhaps soar higher and certainly circle more widely than the orators of England. At heart, though, one must feel, they are as closely akin as they are in language. If our political literature has added anything to the political literature of England, we can hardly assert that it has added more than a demonstration of what that literature might have been in England itself, if in England the constant pressure of external fact had been awhile relaxed.

X

Such relaxation of the pressure of external fact as has seemed to underlie our political thought seems more clearly still to underlie the religious and the philosophical thought of the period we are now considering. The profound truth most emphasized by the Calvinistic creed of the emigrant fathers was the inherent vileness of human nature. Men were born bad, it held, so bad that nothing they themselves could do might ever be enough to save them from deserved damnation. A few generations of native American experience led Americans seriously to question this view of human nature, and in the end to substitute for it one diametrically opposite. In the pure records of New England Unitarianism, in the unfettered philosophy of Emerson, in the half-inspired preaching of the late Bishop of Massachusetts, one cannot help feeling a sublime confidence in the divine possibilities that lie hidden in even the vilest human being.

If we could only induce ourselves honestly to share this confidence, we might be swept with these enthusiasts to ecstatic heights. These men themselves were good men—wonderfully good. They were sympathetic men, permeated with an honest sense of human fraternity. Let us be our best, they seem to say, and all shall be well; and by and by there shall be an end of evil. What is more,—what strengthened their faith and still strengthens their authority,—this noble optimism of theirs was nearer to the truth of human nature about them, for all its growing vileness, than was the grim pessimism of the Calvinist fathers to the human facts of the New World where a whole continent lay open to whoever had courage to penetrate its wilderness. It is only where life is dense that the struggle for existence grows fierce. It is only in a crowded world that we have forced upon us, in all their horror, the lasting realities of sin and evil. In a world where there is still room, whoever will may stand aside, dreaming himself like to a god ; and whoever can put faith in such dreams grows godlike dreaming, and is a very beautiful fact to contemplate. Without the dreamers the world would be poorer : we may all grant that. There are moods— and not our least precious ones—in which, for all our knowledge, the dreamers seem the prophets, revealing the things which are to be.

In the social history of New England there is a petty fact which in moods like this confronts us. It is not unique ; none is more commonplace, none could have been more confidently predicted. Like its innumerable fellows in human experience, though, it has a significance which at moments when we feel like yielding to the ecstasies of optimistic enthusiasm is almost tragic. You must already recognize that generally comic experiment at Brook Farm, where a company of enthusiasts tried to combine plain living, high thinking, and the earning of a decent livelihood. We all know the result. They did not earn a decent livelihood ; they squabbled, in spite of the highest intellectual and moral intentions ; and what few were not dispersed by this state of affairs found plain living by itself not so intrinsically attractive as to prevent them from reverting each to the most comfortable circumstances he could

9

command. Calvinistic depravity in this little circle took no very acute form ; it was enough, however, to prevent successful co-operative aspiration to higher things than every-day life affords.
Brook Farm, in short, typifies what in all likelihood must always happen to American optimists
who try to test their optimism experimentally.
Dreams are very noble things ; but to dream we
must sleep ; and to get along in this actual world
of ours we must be wide awake.

Our business with these dreams, however, is
not to share them for the moment, nor yet to sigh
over their evanescence. It is to ask ourselves
whether they have added to the dreams of England anything which makes richer the lasting expression in English words of the meaning of life.
They have doubtless added something. What this
something is one finds it hard to say ; yet at heart
one can hardly help feeling sure that the records
of human purity would be poorer without the records which the New England dreamers have left
us. Perhaps, as we scrutinize these dreams, their
chief trait seems to be that they are always unfettered yet never base. Left to itself, the devout
free thought of New England has such freedom
from vileness as we love to call childlike. The
dreamers of Old England have been perhaps
more sophisticated, at all events more conscious
of how their dreams must diverge from reality.
In England, we remember, real fact has hardly

relaxed its pressure since English literature began. In America, as we have seen, the case has
hitherto been different. So we find ourselves
where we found ourselves a little while ago, when
we were thumbing anew the leaves of our old
standard speakers. The philosophic dreamers
of America, we must admit, have added to English literature little that might not have been
added in England itself, if in England the pressure of external fact had been awhile relaxed.

XI

So far we have considered these political and
philosophic moods only as they revealed themselves in mere words. We have neglected perhaps their chief manifestation, when for once
they revealed themselves in triumphant action.
In this case they not only expressed themselves ;
they actually altered the course of human history.
A fiery fusion of these moods, which we have
considered apart, was what produced that great
outburst of human sympathy which resulted in the
abolition of African slavery. The forces which
brought about this great result gathered themselves, to no small degree, in literary form. We
all know " Uncle Tom's Cabin ; " we all know the
work of Whittier and of Lowell ; we all know the
passionate intensity of Garrison, the magnificent,
scurrilous eloquence of Phillips. Here, we may

think, is surely something peculiarly our own
—native American enthusiasm dealing with stern
reality, and practically asserting the eternal truth
of humane American optimism. There is no relaxed sense of fact here.

To question this conclusion seems nowadays
almost disloyal. Whatever our personal sympa-
thies, no one can deny the nobly humane impulse
which underlay even the vagaries of Abolition.
Nor can any one deny that what only sixty years
ago was ridiculed as humanitarian fanaticism has
taken its place to-day among the most honoured
traditions of the American people. Abolition
ended what every one now admits to have been
the monstrous evil of negro slavery. For that it
deserves all honour.

Were this the whole story, many of us would
to-day feel more happily secure than we honestly can. To many who pause to think, tradition
seems in this case, as in innumerable others, to
be blinding the eyes of the people to stern, un-
welcome fact. It is hiding the truth that, in the
great days of Abolition as well as now and forever, enthusiasm lacks foresight. It is hiding
the truth that for all their noble enthusiasm, the
Abolitionists, after the good old British fashion,
directed their reforming energies not against the
evils prevalent in the actual society of which they
formed a part ; but against those that prevailed
in a rival society which they knew chiefly by

hearsay. They found this society—and with it our whole country—cursed with the evil of slavery. They left us all burdened with another evil, which at times seems almost as monstrous, almost as untrue to the real facts of human experience. What has supplanted negro slavery is not mere freedom; it is that appalling degradation of American citizenship which the Abolitionists hailed so eagerly under the name of negro suffrage.

In this aspect we cannot so confidently assert that the great movement of Abolition was actuated by a very stern sense of fact. A moment ago, too, we had a glimpse of another aspect in which we may question whether, after all, Abolition was so distinctively American as we like to think. In this aspect, by no means its least obvious, it becomes only one among the many symptoms that prove us still of English race. At least in their modern history, we must remember, the English have displayed inexhaustible power, when impelled by moral motives, of meddling with the business of other people whose affairs they imperfectly understand. We find ourselves, in short, where we found ourselves before. Like the purely political and the purely philosophical literature that surrounds it, the literature of Abolition can hardly be asserted to add much to the lasting expression of the meaning of life otherwise embodied in English words.

XII

WE have dealt now with those kinds of literature whose office is chiefly to affect human conduct. We must turn to those kinds whose office is chiefly to instruct or to delight—to the literature, in short, that we had in mind when at the beginning of this discussion we first thought of the six worthies of New England. With this we shall have to deal even more summarily than with what we have considered before. We may justify ourselves by the thought that while the literature we have touched on is perhaps known chiefly to students, the literature now before us is the literature still most familiar to the American people—the literature, in short, that is sure to be found in any native library, public or private.

A few words, then, of our historians; after that, of our purely literary figures; and we shall have done.

XIII

BOSTON has been the home of historians who may fairly be treated with high respect. One need not name them all, nor need one specifically say that the school for which they stand is not confined to Boston. Once for all, one may affirm that Prescott, and Motley, and the rest, are writers of real industry and real power. According to the methods of their time—a time that

preceded the microscopic accuracy of the scholarship now most in vogue—they collected their
material with diligence and care ; and according
to the pleasantly polite fashion then still prevalent
they expressed the results of this labour in a style
that, despite occasional formality, is permanently
pleasant to read.   What they did, they did well.
They have given us books that should lastingly
hold places in the long list of historical literature
that dignifies English prose.   So much every
one must admit ; and it would be a pleasure to
dwell long on this honourable achievement.

Our business with these men, however, is
only to inquire whether they have added to English literature anything essentially different, in
thought or in phrase, from what that literature
would otherwise comprise ; in other words,
whether they have done work that permanently
enhances our conception of what historical literature may be.   By itself their work is surely
admirable ; but we cannot consider it only by
itself.   It must take its place in a literature
which, to go no further, comprises without it the
work of Gibbon, of Hume, of Macaulay, of Carlyle.
These names are enough.   Admire our own historians as we may, we can claim for them no
higher merit than that of having added their
romantic tales to the already rich store of romantic narrative which without them our language possesses.

XIV

THE word romantic is not very precise. Among a dozen meanings, however, it suggests chiefly, perhaps, a fondness for contemplating things not as they are in our actual life, but rather as they might have been in a dreamy past, or as they might be in some far-off present or fantastic future. No phase of romantic feeling is more constant than that which delights in traditions of things remote in time or in space—if so may be in both. These we may dream of as better, more beautiful, more stirring than the trivialities we know about us. We all know this spirit in the curious petty form which makes native Yankees such minute genealogists ; in that more serious form, too, which makes foreign missions so much more popular than domestic. It was a phase of this spirit, delighting to revive the grandeurs of a vanished time, that impelled Irving, and Ticknor, and Prescott, and Motley to live so much of their inner lives rather among the splendours of Renascent Spain than among the respectable democracy of the United States.

In this aspect the American historians resemble the other American writers whose literary purpose has been more purely artistic. The dominant note in the work of almost all of these may be called romantic. It was a phase of the romantic spirit that impelled Irving again, and

Longfellow, and Lowell, and at times even Whittier, to saturate themselves in the delights of great European literature; and to phrase this experience in terms that, however modern fashion may sometimes slight them, have made romantic dreams the lasting possession of American youth. To no European, indeed, can Europe, with its limitless past, be quite so stirring as to a native of this New World, in whom a starved romantic spirit is lurking; and nothing has more helped us to this keenest, purest kind of pleasure than our romantic historians, and poets, and novelists. Whoever does not love and enjoy them must be inappreciative or ungrateful.

They have done us, then, a great service—a service on which it would be pleasant to dwell long. Here, however, we have no time for eulogy. The question before us is simply whether they have made English literature more widely, lastingly expressive than it would have been without them. In all frankness we can hardly assert that on the whole they have. Without them English literature possesses records enough and to spare that show what the romantic spirit is. These records, as well as our own, must be in mind whenever we attempt, as we attempted a moment ago, to define this spirit. The definition was unhappily crude and vague. It was enough, though, to fix one fact: in essence the romantic spirit is dreamy, and like a true dream flourishes best when the pressure of external fact is deliberately or accidentally relaxed. The difference between our romantic literature and the romantic literature of Europe is not great ; it lies chiefly, perhaps, in the fact that, with perceptibly less intensity and power, ours is less conscious, more spontaneous. As we consider our romantic writers coolly, in short, they generally reveal themselves just as English-speaking men, happily resident in a world where troublesome fact presses more lightly than in England.

XV

AMONG them, however, there are two, very unlike each other, who are similar in being distinctly different from any writers whom we can feel to be characteristically English. These are Poe and Hawthorne.

Poe, to be sure, is fantastic and meretricious throughout. In his work as in his life he was haunted by the vices and the falsity of the stage that bred him ; but he was really haunted. As one knows him better, one does not love him more. In another way, though, one grows to care for him, or at least to pity him. For with all his falsity, with all his impudence and sham, the man is a man by himself. There is something freakish, not quite earthly, wholly his own in the fancies and the cadences that grow wild amid his work. If it be something to have added a new note to literature, then we Americans must respect the memory of Poe.

With Hawthorne, the case is very different. To men of our time, beyond doubt, his work seems generally not fantastic but imaginative, and surely not meretricious but in its own way beautiful. Nor is this the whole story : almost alone among our writers, we may say, Hawthorne has a lasting native significance. For this there are surely two good reasons. In the first place, he is almost the solitary American artist who has phrased his meaning in words of which the beauty seems sure to grow with the years. In the second place, what marks him as most impregnably American is this : when we look close to see what his meaning really was, we find it a thing that in the old days, at last finally dead and gone, had been the great motive power of his race. What Hawthorne really voices is that strange, morbid, haunting sense of other things that we see or hear, which underlay the intense idealism of the emigrant Puritans, and which remains perhaps the most inalienable emotional heritage of their children. It is Hawthorne, in brief, who finally phrases the meaning of such a life as Theophilus Eaton lived and Cotton Mather recorded.

Hawthorne and Poe, then, have added something, in both thought and phrase, to the literature of England. Yet when we ask ourselves

coolly just what this something is, we need not
be surprised to find no very new answer. In the
half-mad vagaries of the one, and in the melancholy musings of the other, we can feel, to be
sure, at least emotions that we should have far
to seek elsewhere. In the very extravagance of
their freedom, however, these emotions bring us
back to where we have so often found ourselves
before. They are surely such as we should expect dreamy, imaginative, English-speaking folks
to know, when their lot is cast in a still un-
crowded world. For all this, though, Poe and
Hawthorne are in no wise Englishmen. Whatever they express, it is surely something of their
own, and so of ours.

XVI

SOMETHING of our own, too, is expressed by the
kind of literature that foreigners are apt to think
most characteristically American. This is the
sort of thing that is called American humour. In
trivial forms it pervades the newspapers. Its
vulgar heroes are Artemas Ward and Josh Bill-
ings. Its masterpieces are probably to be found
in Irving's "Knickerbocker," and in the works
of Lowell, and of the last survivor of the best
days of New England letters—Dr. Holmes.

One can hardly define American humour, but
we all know what it is. It is based on shrewd,
cool, good-tempered common-sense ; it has serene

assurance, it has great freshness of feeling. One likes it, one laughs at it, and above all one feels it generally spontaneous and wholesome. It leaves no bitterness behind. Somehow, though, it is not profound humour, not great; it is apt to have less serious relation to life than at first glance seems the case. With all its fresh charm, all its wholesome humanity, its final trait seems, broadly speaking, to be good-natured, reckless extravagance of both thought and phrase. This extravagance, if it be really the chief trait of our humour, marks even this most characteristic phase of our national literature as expressing only another aspect of the same experience that we have found so generally to underlie what we, as a people, have thought, and felt, and said. At bottom, after all, extravagance is only another name for cheerful neglect of stern reality. It is another and a brighter expression of what men know and feel when external fact does not press them too hard.

XVII

So much for the American literature of the past. This is not the place to deal with the present or the future. In the period we have considered, almost every writer has been concerned either with what had gone before him or with what was passing about him. Almost all, in short, have expressed what we have seen to be the historical experience of American life—the manner of the free growth of an English people in a world where there was still plenty of room.

In this same period, however, there is a single figure who seems steadily and constantly to face not what is now past, but what is now present or to come. Though his right to respect is questioned oftenest of all, we cannot fairly pass Walt Whitman without mention. He lacks, of course, to a grotesque degree, artistic form ; but that very lack is characteristic. Artistic form, as we have seen, is often the final stamp that marks human expression as a thing of the past. Whitman remarkably illustrates this principle : he lacks form chiefly because he is stammeringly overpowered by his bewildering vision of what he believes to be the future. He is uncouth, inarticulate, whatever you please that is least orthodox ; yet, after all, he can make you feel for the moment how even the ferry-boats plying from New York to Brooklyn are fragments of God's eternities. Those of us who love the past are far from sharing his confidence in the future. Surely, however, that is no reason for denying the miracle that he has wrought by idealizing the East River. The man who has done this is the only one who points out the stuff of which perhaps the new American literature of the future may in time be made, who foreruns perhaps a spirit that may inspire that literature, if it grow at last into an organic form of its own, with a meaning not to be sought in other worlds than this western world of ours.

XVIII

BRIEF and hasty as this sketch has had to be, few as are the aspects of our life and our letters on which we have had time to touch, it has perhaps been enough to indicate what some of us have meant when in careless phrase we have sometimes said that America has no literature at all. What we really mean is only that while Americans have added something to the lasting expressions of the meaning of life that are phrased in English words, they are still far from having added enough to justify a valid claim to an independent place among those peoples whose national literatures are inevitably lasting possessions of humanity. New England, in its own little way, has voiced the experience of English humanity free for awhile from the stern pressure of external fact. That is almost all.

Nor can I feel that we have erred, while considering American literature, in attending chiefly to that New England which to me is the spot on earth where life means most. In America, I believe, only New England has expressed itself in a literary form which inevitably commands attention from whoever pursues such inquiries as ours. What else has been written in the periods of American life that we have considered may almost certainly be brought within generalizations based on the literature of New England. In this fact a New Englander feels a pride deeper than I realized when I began to write these lines; yet he feels, too, a sadness. By the inexorable law on which we have touched more than once, the very fact that New England has actually expressed its unfettered experience seems to mean that the unfettered experience of New England, and all the New England that we have known and cared for, is past or passing.

Yet after all, much as we may love it, even that unfettered New England is not the ultimate fact of human history. It is hard to avoid the conviction that this very New England we love so well has youthfully overestimated herself and her work. In endeavouring not unduly to praise this work, then, many of us perhaps err the other way. So far as it goes, this work is sound and wholesome. What the six worthies with whose names we began this discussion have contributed to lasting literature is no great thing, to be sure; but it is something. Something better still is the great purity of their lives. Emasculate we may call them in certain moods. In other moods, and better, their lives tell us that if restraint be relaxed what will flourish most in English human nature is not the evil; and whatever else, great

or little, their works tell us, they tell us nothing
sordid, base, impure.   As the struggling years
of the future come upon us, we shall value this
purity more and more.   In the past many of us
have looked at these men with irreverent impatience.   What have they done, after all, we have
asked, that we should so trouble ourselves about
them.   But now, as the years are passing, we ask
ourselves such questions less and less.   Rather
we look at these men with growing love and
veneration.   For the little group is a group that
we should have far to seek elsewhere.   Of each
one may be said the truest and the loveliest thing
that has been said of Longfellow—and no man
could wish a worthier epitaph :

" He left his native air the sweeter for his song."

10

VI

JOHN GREENLEAF WHITTIER

(A Memoir presented to the American Academy of Arts and Sciences, on June 14, 1893.)

JOHN GREENLEAF WHITTIER

I

JOHN GREENLEAF WHITTIER was born in Haverhill, Massachusetts, on December 17, 1807.* His
ancestors, in every line of the soundest Yankee
stock, had resided from the earliest times in Essex County, or in the older regions of New Hampshire. The house in which he was born had been
built by his emigrant ancestor, Thomas Whittier,
who died at the age of seventy-six, in 1696, after
above fifty years' residence in New England. In
1694, Joseph Whittier, son of the emigrant, and
great-grandfather of the poet, had married the
daughter of a well-known Quaker. Probably
from this time the immediate family of the poet
had belonged to the Religious Society of Friends.
In all other respects their condition had been
that of substantial New England farmers.

Amid the extreme diversity of religious views
that marks our own time, and the efforts now so
general among the New England clergy to emphasize the few things that religious people be-

* For the facts of Whittier's life I rely chiefly on the
biography by Mr. F. H. Underwood.

lieve in common, and to neglect the many concerning which they radically differ, we are apt to
think of religious divergences as verbal or formal. In general we are probably right. Modern
Yankees, at all events, are not profound theologians. They are disposed either to take religion
as they find it, or else without much ado to select in place of their ancestral faith some creed
or form of worship which they find socially or
æsthetically more congenial. Sectarian differences nowadays certainly do not display themselves in obvious differences of character. With
people of ordinary parts, of course, this has generally been the case at all times; with really
serious natures the case is different. The few
people in any generation who seem instinctively
aware of the tremendous seriousness of religion—
the people whose presence in this world was perhaps the chief basis of the Calvinistic doctrine
of election—are inevitably affected, often perma-
mently, by the religious doctrine that surrounds
their early years. Whatever else Whittier was,
he was a profoundly religious man, who could not
help taking life in earnest. To understand him
at all, then, we must know something of the
peculiar religious views which he never relin-
quished.

II

THE Friends in New England, writes a gentleman who is now an earnest member of the Religious Society in question,

"were Orthodox in that they believed in God as Father, Son, and Holy Spirit, in Christ as truly one with the Father, yet also very man, and in the efficacy of His atonement for the forgiveness of sins. But the term 'Orthodox' in New England is usually taken to mean the tenets of the Westminster Confession. Whittier was trained to regard the extreme views of this Confession with aversion. He drank in the truth of the universal love of God to all men in Christian, Jewish, or Pagan lands, that God so *loved* the *world* that He sent His Son, that Christ died for *all* men, and His atonement availed for all who in every land accepted the light with which He enlightened their minds and consciences, and who listening to His still small voice in the soul turned in any true sense toward God, away from evil and to the right and loving. Whittier thus drank in a spirit of universal love, a sense of oneness with all men, that fitted him to espouse and advocate the cause of the ignorant, the weak, the outcast—the slave, the Indian, the heathen. It gave him sympathy with all loving, saintly souls like Fénelon, Guion, and other Roman Catholics of like spirit, and nerved his manly, indignant scorn of hard and cruel men that professed the name of 'Christian.' Whittier was trained to have a great reverence for the Bible. . . . He had read much in the Journals of Friends. He had steeped his mind with their thoughts and loved them because they were so saintly and yet so humbly unconscious of it.

"The title 'Quaker Poet' is a true one, not simply because he was a Friend by membership, but because he was permeated by the spirit of Quaker Christianity. It is true that Whittier was much broadened by association with men like Emerson, Longfellow, and others, Garrison especially; but he was to the end a Friend in his religion."

The letter from which these passages are quoted was addressed to a kinswoman of Whittier's, who has kindly sent me some notes of her own recollections of Friends. Though some years younger than he, she was trained under similar influences. Her recollections, then, we may guess in some degree to have blended with his.

"During the early part of this century," she writes, " I think the Society of Friends throughout the rural districts of New England retained in a great measure the stern, rigid simplicity and exclusiveness which characterized the religious people of the old Puritan days. They were thoroughly Orthodox,* and gave little heed to the Unitarian controversy among others. . . . Friends then had not, I think, *all* the aggressive fervor of the earlier days; there was a degree of lukewarmness; but they had among them many ministers,† untrained in the learning of the world, but full of spiritual life, who laboured not only among Friends, but wherever they felt themselves called.

"The Discipline of the Society was rigidly observed by most. Queries were answered Quarterly, and looked after by appointed Committee. I will give some of the Queries,

* *i.e.*, Trinitarian Christians, but not Calvinists.

† Among the Friends in general, men and women may alike be ministers; but a minister may receive no salary.

as they undoubtedly exerted some influence over the children, who often listened to them:

"Are meetings for worship duly attended? hour* observed? Are they preserved from sleeping or other unbecoming behavior?

"Are the Holy Scriptures frequently read?

"Do [Friends] avoid spirituous liquors except for Medicine?

"Do they avoid unnecessary frequenting of taverns or other places of public resort?

"Are the poor looked after, and assisted in such business as they are capable of?

"Are [Friends] careful to inspect their affairs, punctual in promises?

"Do they live within the bounds of their income?

"Do they deal with offenders in the Spirit of Meekness? etc., etc.

"The children of Friends were early taught that there was a still small voice given them by their Heavenly Father which could tell them when they were doing wrong. †

"In most cases they were taken regularly to meetings for Worship—often to those for Discipline—where they had to sit still on hard benches. They had no Sabbath-schools, but in almost all families on First Day afternoon the children were required to listen to readings in the Holy Scriptures and they were generally well informed in all Bible History. When Whittier was a little boy he once remarked he thought David could not have been a Friend, as he was a man of war.

* *i.e.* If no one feels called to speak, do they regularly wait for at least one hour in silence?

† This doctrine of universal conscience seems the fundamental one of the Society of Friends.

"Music and dancing were not indulged in. Novels were forbidden. But they all the more enjoyed Milton, Young, Cowper, and histories when obtainable. It seems Whittier had none of these, at which I marvel, as his grandmother, who lived with them, was a Greenleaf, and they were literary people."

Without actually quoting these notes, so kindly sent me, I could hardly have reproduced the effect they make on one who carefully reads them. To restate in one's own words the earnest faith they so tenderly express seems unsympathetic. In more worldly phrase than theirs, however, what Whittier was taught and believed seems to have been this : To all human beings God has given an inner light, to all He speaks with a still small voice. Follow the light, obey the voice, and all will be well. Evil-doers are they who neglect the light and the voice. Now the light and the voice are God's, so to all who will attend they must ultimately show the same truth. If the voice call us to correct others, then, or the light shine upon manifest evil, it is God's will that we smite error, if so may be by revealing truth. If those who err be Friends, our duty bids us expostulate with them ; and if they be obdurate, to present them for discipline, which may result in their exclusion from our Religious Society. The still small voice, it seems, really warns everybody that certain lines of conduct are essentially wrong —among which are the drinking of spirits, the frequenting of taverns, indulgence in gaming, the use of oaths, and the enslavement of any human being.

III

In this firm faith, fortified from Scripture, that everybody really knows right from wrong, that many common lines of conduct are indubitably wrong, and that whoever follow such lines of conduct do so from wilful neglect of the inner light and the still small voice divinely vouchsafed them, Whittier was trained and lived. To this faith, involving the essential equality of all mankind, and the deliberate ungodliness of whoever by word or deed fails to recognize this equality, may be traced many of the peculiar characteristics which make him, even to those who mistrust the reforms in which he so passionately engaged himself, perhaps the least irritating of reformers. Not only was he trained from infancy in this faith, of which reform is the only logical expression in action; but his life from beginning to end was singularly remote from that heart-breaking experience of actual fact, in crowded and growing communities, which goes so far nowadays to disprove, for whoever will frankly recognize what is before him, the essential vitality of those parts of human nature which are best.

A barefoot boy to look at, an unswerving believer at heart in the inner light of the Friends, and by nature one of those calmly passionate Yankees who cannot help taking life in earnest, he grew up in days when the New England country was still pure in the possession of an unmixed race whose power of self-government has never been surpassed. His "Snow-Bound" relates his own memories of childhood ; some of the sketches preserved in his prose works * add pleasant touches to the better-known pictures in his verse.   He always had a hankering for literature. A strolling Scotch vagrant, hospitably treated to cheese and cider, sang him in payment some songs of Burns.   At fourteen he laid hands on a copy of Burns's poems. These seem to have started him at writing.   At seventeen he had written a poem on the "Exile's Departure" from the "shores of Hibernia," † which in 1826 found its way into print in the Newburyport *Free Press*, then edited by William Lloyd Garrison.   From 1827 to 1892 he passed no year without writing verses which sooner or later came to publication. In 1826, before he was nineteen years old, he was visited while at work in the corn-field by Garrison, the young editor, who had been struck by the merit of his verses.   The friendship thus be-

---

* Notably "Yankee Gypsies," and "Magicians and Witch Folk, " Prose Works, i., 326, 399.

† Poetical Works, iv., 333.   This poem, like that on the "Vale of the Merrimac" cited below, which belongs to the same year, suggests the influence of Moore.

gun proved life-long. Had anything been needed to enhance the reformatory instincts of a Yankee Quaker, the chance that this first literary recognition came from the man destined to be the most strenuous reformer of his time would have been enough.

In his twentieth year Whittier went to the Academy in Haverhill, where he spent two terms, and particularly distinguished himself in English composition. During a winter vacation he taught a country school. At twenty-one he was already a professional writer for some of the smaller newspapers. At twenty-three he was editor of the *Haverhill Gazette ;* and before he was twenty-four he was made editor of the *New England Weekly Review*, a paper published at Hartford, Connecticut. At the end of a year and a half he resigned this office, on the ground of ill-health, and returned to Massachusetts. Meanwhile he had published a small volume of " New England Legends."

At this time Garrison had just established the *Liberator* in Boston. The movement for the abolition of slavery was fairly begun. Into this movement Whittier threw himself with all his might. For thirty years he constantly advocated it in both prose and verse. He was a member of the Anti-Slavery Convention at Philadelphia, in 1833.* He was attacked by a mob at Haverhill in

* See his vivid reminiscences of it; Prose Works, iii., 171.

1834 ; and by a worse one at Concord, New Hampshire, in 1835. In this year he was for one term a member of the General Court of Massachusetts. In 1837 he went to New York, as a secretary of the National Anti-Slavery Society. Early in 1838 he was made editor of the *Pennsylvania Freeman*, a journal devoted to the cause of abolition, published at Philadelphia. In May, 1838, the office of this paper, together with Pennsylvania Hall, just erected for the purpose of providing the Abolitionists with a regular place of meeting, was burned by a mob. In 1840 he resigned his charge of the *Freeman*, and rejoined his mother and sister, who had moved to Amesbury, Massachusetts. Here henceforth was his legal residence.

From this time on, his life was remarkably uneventful. Shy in temperament, and generally troubled by that sort of robust poor health which frequently accompanies total abstinence, he lived secluded in the Yankee country for the better part of fifty-two years. He wrote a great deal ; but rarely, it is said, above half an hour at a time.* In 1849 a collection of his poems was published ; in 1857 came another, this time from his final publishers, Ticknor & Fields.† He had

* My authority for this is a little monograph by Mrs. J. T. Fields.

† The firm's name has changed several times. It is now Houghton, Mifflin & Company.

now become a recognized literary figure. He was concerned in the starting of the *Atlantic Monthly*. The temper of the North was beginning at last to favour Abolition. In the civil war, dreadful as such an event was to his religious convictions, he saw the hand of God destroying the great evil of slavery. He had always adhered to that branch of the Anti-slavery party which believed in opposing the national evil by regular political means. He was an ardent member of the Republican party. The close of the war, which found his principles victorious, found him in popular estimation a great man.

In 1871 he was made a Fellow of the American Academy of Arts and Sciences.* It is not remembered that he ever attended a meeting. General society, even in its severer forms, he never found congenial. An occasional visit to intimate friends in Boston, and of a summer to the Isles of Shoals, or later to the hill country about Chocorua, were the chief incidents in his life. For all this superficial repose, however, he never stopped writing. His " Birthday Greeting," sent to Dr. Holmes on August 29, 1892, was written only a few weeks before his death. He died, in his eighty-fifth year, at Hampton Falls, New Hampshire, on September 7, 1892.

* By whose kindness I am permitted to reprint this memoir from their Proceedings.

IV

DURING his last years he made a final collection of his writings, with a few brief notes.* It is in seven volumes, four of verse and three of prose. The arrangement is a little confusing. He classified his works under a number of not very definite heads; and under each head printed his material chronologically. The first volume contains "Narrative and Legendary Poems," from 1830 to 1888; the second contains "Poems of Nature," from 1830 to 1886, "Poems Subjective and Reminiscent," from 1841 to 1887, and "Religious Poems," from 1830 to 1886; the third contains "Anti-slavery Poems," beginning with one to William Lloyd Garrison, in 1832, and ending with one to his memory, in 1879, and "Songs of Labor and Reform," from 1838 to 1887; the fourth contains "Personal Poems," from 1834 to 1886, "Occasional Poems," from 1852 to 1888, and reprints of the "Tent on the Beach," originally published in 1867, and of his last volume, "At Sundown," which originally appeared shortly after his death. In an Appendix are some youthful poems, written as early as 1825. The prose works are classified in a similarly confusing way. There is a volume of "Tales and Sketches," including his essay in his-

* "The Writings of John Greenleaf Whittier." Riverside Press: 1893.

torical fiction, "Margaret Smith's Journal in the Province of Massachusetts Bay, 1678–9;" a volume of "Old Portraits and Modern Sketches," "Personal Sketches and Tributes," and "Historical Papers;" and a volume concerning the "Conflict with Slavery," "Reform and Politics," "The Inner Life," and "Criticism."

This bewildering arrangement of the work of sixty-seven years is characteristic. By far the longest article in any of the seven volumes is "Margaret Smith's Journal," which covers one hundred and eighty-six pages. By far the greater part of all the work consists of verses or papers which could easily have been written at a short sitting. Uncertain health, the early practice of journalism, and the lack of that higher education which demands prolonged intellectual effort in a single direction seem to have combined in preventing the power of sustained literary labor. As he writes of himself: *

" His good was mainly an intent,
    His evil not of forethought done ;
  The work he wrought was rarely meant
    Or finished as begun.

    .   .   .   .

" The words he spake, the thoughts he penned,
    Are mortal as his hand and brain,
  But if they serve the Master's end,
    He has not lived in vain."

* " My Namesake," Poetical Works, ii., 118, 121.

11

That last stanza is unduly modest.   There are
passages in Whitter's works which have strength
and merit of a kind that ought to survive.   Of
his works as wholes, however, his criticism is
true.   There is hardly one in which the vital passages are not half-buried in irrelevance, redund-
ance, or common-place.   The very confusion in
which he finally presented his writings to posterity is typical of his inability to handle anything on a large scale.

V

To one who, amid this confusion, sets himself
to discover the characteristic traits of the work,
the first salient features are not its merits.   Whittier was certainly precocious.   Certainly, too, the
power he displayed in youth did not meet the
common fate of precocity.   But the change from
his earliest work to his latest is surprisingly
slight.   At seventeen he wrote, of the Merrimac : *

> " Oh, lovely the scene, when the gray misty vapour
>   Of morning is lifted from Merrimac's shore ;
> When the firefly, lighting his wild gleaming taper,
>   The dimly seen lowlands comes glimmering o'er ;

* Poetical Works, iv., 336.   In the rhythm the influence
of Moore seems marked.

When on thy calm surface the moonbeam falls brightly,
  And the dull bird of night is his covert forsaking,
When the whippoorwill's notes from thy margin sound
      lightly,
  And break on the sound which thy small waves are
      making."

At thirty-three he wrote of it again : *

    " But look ! the yellow light no more
      Streams down on wave and verdant shore ;
      And clearly on the calm air swells
      The twilight voice of distant bells.
      From Ocean's bosom, white and thin,
      The mists come slowly rolling in ;
      Hills, woods, the river's rocky rim
      Amidst the sea-like vapour swim,
      While yonder lonely coast-light, set
      Within its wave-washed minaret,
      Half-quenched, a beamless star and pale,
      Shines dimly through its cloudy veil ! "

At fifty-nine he wrote of the light-house visible from Hampton Beach : †

          " Just then the ocean seemed
      To lift a half-faced moon in sight ;
      And shoreward o'er the waters gleamed,
      From crest to crest, a line of light.
        .   .   .   .
    " Silently for a space each eye
      Upon that sudden glory turned :
      Cool from the land the breeze blew by,
      The tent-ropes flapped, the long beach churned

            * Poetical Works, ii., 12.
            † Ibid., iv., 281.

Its waves to foam ; on either hand
Stretched, far as sight, the hills of sand ;
    With bays of marsh, and capes of bush and tree,
    The woods black shore-line loomed beyond the
        meadowy sea."

And as he dealt with Nature here, for above forty years simply looking and telling just what he saw, so he dealt with everything from beginning to end.   For sixty-seven years his work retains its chief characteristics with remarkably slight alteration.

The most salient of these characteristics, as I have said, are not the merits.   The lines just cited have an obvious air of commonplace.   It is deceptive.   As one grows to know them, and the hundreds of others for which we must let them stand, one begins insensibly to realize that the power of selective observation which underlies them is of no common order.   Commonplace, however, they surely look ; and commonplace beyond all doubt are endless passages throughout Whittier's verse.   The man lacked the saving grace of humour.   In all the seven volumes I have found but one passage that really amused me : this is an account in "Yankee Gypsies" * of how a drunken vagabond broke into the Whittier homestead when the men were away, and made formal love to the dismayed grandmother, who was born

* Prose Works, i., 339.

Greenleaf.   In Whittier's verse his lack of humour is sometimes startling.   In a poem * where
a Yankee stage-driver describes the profoundly
gracious merits of a passenger who once made
him stop while she sketched a panoramic view,
occurs this stanza :

> " ' As good as fair ; it seemed her joy
>   To comfort and to give ;
>   My poor, sick wife, and cripple boy,
>   Will bless her while they live ! '
>   The tremor in the driver's tone
>   His manhood did not shame :
>   ' I dare say, sir, you may have known —— '
>   He named a well-known name."

And in a poem † commemorating a railway conductor who lost his life in an accident, come
these passages :

> " Lo ! the ghastly lips of pain,
>   Dead to all thought save duty's, moved again :
>   ' Put out the signals for the other train ! ' "

> " No nobler utterance since the world began
>   From lips of saint or martyr ever ran,
>   Electric, through the sympathies of man.

> .   .   .   .

> " Others he saved, himself he could not save.

> " Nay, the lost life *was* saved.   He is not dead
>   Who in his record still the earth shall tread
>   With God's clear aureole shining round his head."

* " The Hill-Top ; " Poetical Works, iv., 58.
† " Conductor Bradley ; " Poetical Works, i., 359.

The noble simplicity of this second passage does something to atone for the appalling literalness and the monstrous hyperbole of the first. One cannot help wondering, though, whether any other writer of real merit than Whittier would ever have deliberately reprinted such passages side by side.

His lack of humour, then, was serious. So, to a less degree, was his lack of artistic feeling. The remarkably narrow range of his metrical forms, the astonishing errors of his rhymes are familiar features of his verse. Another defect, too, must have been apparent to whoever has read even the passages already quoted. He had little strength of creative imagination. His poetical figures are almost always both obvious and trite. A light-house resembles a minaret; the woods bordering a salt meadow are like the shore bordering the actual sea; a good man, when dead, is provided with an aureole; and so on. The moralizing passages frequent throughout his work display the same weakness. If in his lack of humour he sinks below the commonplace, there is nothing in the technical form of his work, or in the creative power of his imagination, which often rises above it.

VI

YET as one grows to know the work of Whittier, one grows insensibly to feel that essentially it is

far from commonplace, that it really deserves the
importance accorded it in contemporary literature, that no small part of it will probably out-
live the age to which it was addressed, and perhaps even the work of any other contemporary
American.   I have purposely touched on his
faults, and put them all together.   Not to have
recognized them would have been deliberately
not to see him as he was.   In growing to know
his work, these are what one first remarks.   By
and by one finds them forgotten in a sense that
this poet, whom one has grown to know, has
in him lasting elements for which greatness
is perhaps no undue name.   Throughout the
work of his sixty-seven years one feels with
growing admiration a constant simplicity of feeling and of phrase, as pure as the country air he
loved to breathe.   One feels, too, constant, unswerving purity of nature, of motive, of life.
And if one feel, too, the limits of thought and
of experience that made such purity and simplicity possible throughout eighty-five years of
human existence, one is none the sadder for that.
What Whittier voiced was a life that could be
lived in our own New England through the
stormiest years of the Nineteenth Century.   Limited though it were, that life throughout, in
thought, in feeling, in word, in act, was simple
and pure—commonplace, if you will, in more
aspects than one, but in one never commonplace :

never for a moment was it ignoble. It has been
the fortune of New England, above other parts of
our country, to fix the standards and the ideals
that have hitherto prevailed throughout the continent of North America. There is courage in
the thought that even in our own time New
England could bring forth and sustain such noble
purity as his.

To feel how genuine, how pure, how noble the
man was, with all his limits, we must consider his
work in some detail. His own classification of
it, as we have seen, is confusing. His prose work,
once for all, is of little importance. It shows
him possessed of a quietly pleasant narrative style,
and of a controversial style which has considerable force. It phrases little or nothing, however,
that is not equally phrased in his more favourite
vehicle of verse. We may best consider, then,
chiefly his verse: first, that part of it which most
reveals himself; then, that which deals with his
own experience of Nature; then, his romantic narratives; and finally, the work which he himself
deemed most important—his life-long advocacy
of human freedom.

VII

If masterpiece be not an extravagant term for
any work of Whittier's, we may perhaps call
"Snow-Bound"* his masterpiece. At fifty-seven,

* Poetical Works, ii., 134–159.

when almost all of his immediate family were
dead, he wrote in tenderly simple verse this record of his earliest memories. " Flemish pictures
of old days," he calls it toward the end. The
phrase would be apt, but that it ignores what
seems to me the most notable trait of all. Flemish pictures one thinks of as pictures of a peas-
antry. In " Snow-Bound " we have a country-
folk very rare in human history. No life could
be much simpler, much more remote from lux-
urious comfort or lazy ease than the life that is
pictured here; but for all their brave rusticity
these sturdy Yankees, toiling in summer on their
rocky farms, resting perforce in such winter
moments as buried them in almost Arctic snow-
drifts, are no peasants. What makes them what
they are is that they are still lords of themselves
and of the soil they till. Simple with all the
simplicity of hereditary farming folk, they are at
the same time gentle with the unconscious grace
of people who are aware of no earthly superiors.
This is the phase of human nature that Whittier
knew first and best. This is what he assumed
and believed that all mankind might be. Very
surely, too, this is the stuff of which any sound
democracy must be made. So, of this stormy
evening, he writes :

> " Shut in from all the world without,
>   We sat the clean-winged hearth about,

Content to let the north-wind roar
In baffled rage at pane and door,
While the red logs before us beat
The frost-line back with tropic heat;
And ever, when a louder blast
Shook beam and rafter as it passed,
The merrier up its roaring draught
The great throat of the chimney laughed;
The house-dog on his paws outspread
Laid to the fire his drowsy head,
The cat's dark silhouette on the wall
A couchant tiger's seemed to fall;
And, for the winter fireside meet,
Between the andirons' straggling feet,
The mug of cider * simmered slow,
The apples sputtered in a row,
And, close at hand, the basket stood
With nuts from brown October's wood.''

This vivid simplicity of description is generally recognized. Less obvious and less certainly known is the occasional ultimate simplicity of phrase which makes certain lines † in '' Snow-Bound'' notable. Take this reference to those that are no more :

'' We turn the pages that they read,
  Their written words we linger o'er,
  But *in the sun they cast no shade*,
  No voice is heard, no sign is made,
  No step is on the conscious floor ! ''

*It has generally been customary in New England, I am told, not to deem cider spirituous.

† In the following passages the italics are mine.

Again, take this couplet about the maiden aunt, so familiar a figure in New England households:

> " All unprofaned she held apart
> The virgin fancies of the heart."

Again, these lines, for once imaginative:

> " How many a poor one's blessing went
> With thee beneath *the low green tent*
> *Whose curtain never outward swings.*"

Again:

> " But still I wait with ear and eye
> For something gone that should be nigh,
> *A loss in all familiar things,*
> In flower that blooms, and bird that sings."

Again still:

> " And while in life's late afternoon,
> Where cool and long the shadows grow,
> I walk to meet *the night that soon*
> *Shall shape and shadow overflow,*
> I cannot feel that thou art far."

It was from such memories as these, thus remembered, that he went to his work in this world. The very first poem in his class of " Subjective and Reminiscent " suggests, too, what rarely appears in his writing, that he had tender memories, of a less domestic nature. For these verses, addressed at the age of twenty-three to a lady of

Calvinistic tendencies, from whom he seems to
have been long parted, contain this passage : *

> " Ere this, thy quiet eye hath smiled
>   My picture of thy youth to see,
> When, half a woman, half a child,
> Thy very artlessness beguiled,
>   *And folly's self seemed wise in thee.*"

His chief work, as we have seen, he believed to
be the work of reform. The personal effects of
such work he felt sensibly. At thirty-five he
wrote of himself for a lady's album :†

> " A banished name from Fashion's sphere,
>   A lay unheard of Beauty's ear,
>   Forbid, disowned,—what do they here ? "

At forty-five, in lines to his Namesake,‡ he draws
his own portrait :

> " Some blamed him, some believed him good ;
>   The truth lay doubtless 'twixt the two ;
> He reconciled as best he could
>   Old faith and fancies new.

> .   .   .   .

> " He loved his friends, forgave his foes ;
>   And, if his words were harsh at times,
> He spared his fellow-men,—his blows
>   Fell only on their crimes.

* " Memories "; Poetical Works, ii., 96.
† " Ego " ; Poetical Works, ii., 102.
‡ Poetical Works, ii., 116.

"He loved the great and wise, but found
   His human heart to all akin
Who met him on the common ground
   Of suffering and sin.

.   .   .   .

"Ill served his tides of feeling strong
   To turn the common mills of use ;
And, over restless wings of song,
   His birthright garb hung loose !

"His eye was beauty's powerless slave,
   And his the ear which discord pains ;
Few guessed beneath his aspect grave
   What passions strove in chains.

.   .   .   .   .   .

"He worshipped as his fathers did,
   And kept the faith of childish days,
And, howsoe'er he strayed or slid,
   He loved the good old ways—

"The simple tastes, the kindly traits,
   The tranquil air, and gentle speech,
The silence of the soul that waits
   For more than man to teach.

.   .   .   .   .   .

"And listening with his forehead bowed,
   Heard the Divine compassion fill
The pauses of the trump and cloud
   With whispers small and still."

However his actual belief may have been affected
by the immense growth of devout free thought

about him, he never for a moment faltered in faith that the inner light of the Friends is real. On his sixty-fourth birthday, he wrote : *

"God is, and all is well !

"His light shines on me from above,
   His low voice speaks within,—
The patience of immortal love
   Outwearying mortal sin."

And again, at seventy-eight : †

"By all that He requires of me,
   I know what God himself must be.

"No picture to my aid I call,
   I shape no image in my prayer ;
I only know in Him is all
   Of life, light, beauty, everywhere."

In his last volume are some lines‡ which must have been written about this time, concerning an outdoor reception, where some young girls had pleased him :

"But though I feel, with Solomon,
   'Tis pleasant to behold the sun,
I would not if I could repeat
A life which still is good and sweet ;

* "My Birthday"; Poetical Works, ii., 164.
† "Revelation"; Poetical Works, ii., 343.
‡ "An Outdoor Reception"; Poetical Works, iv., 297.

I keep in age, as in my prime,
A not uncheerful step with time.

.   .   .   .   .   .

" On easy terms with law and fate,
For what must be I calmly wait,
And trust the path I cannot see,—
That God is good sufficeth me."

VIII

WITH less quotation we could hardly have appreciated the effect of Whittier's personality that emerges from these self-expressive poems. Superficially commonplace in their simplicity, they really express a character in which the simple virtues of New England are so firmly rooted that by very force of its unassuming strength it becomes strongly individual. It is pervaded, however, with true Yankee melancholy, for which, so far as we have yet seen, there was no help but what might be found in fervent religion and its accompanying duties. Throughout life, however, Whittier had another resource. To quote once more from the poem to his namesake, from which I have already quoted much :

" Yet Heaven was kind, and here a bird
And there a flower beguiled his way ;
And, cool, in summer noons, he heard
The fountains plash and play.

"On all his sad or restless moods
  The patient peace of Nature stole ;
The quiet of the fields and woods
  Sank deep into his soul."

In other words, Whittier found in the contemplation of New England landscape the most constant, lasting pleasure of his life.

In his collected works, the poems he classifies as "of Nature" fill only eighty-six pages. In reality, poetry of Nature pervades his whole work. Under this head, for example, may clearly fall the first lines to the Merrimac which I quoted,* and the passage concerning night-fall on Hampton Beach,† as well as a great part of "Snow-Bound." Yet all these are classified elsewhere. So are numberless passages like the following, which to his mind is apparently either narrative or legendary : ‡

" Along the roadside, like the flowers of gold
  The tawny Incas for their gardens wrought,
Heavy with sunshine droops the golden-rod,
And the red pennons of the cardinal-flowers
Hang motionless upon their upright staves.
The sky is hot and hazy, and the wind,
Wing-weary with its long flight from the south,
Unfelt ; yet, closely scanned, yon maple leaf
With faintest motion, as one stirs in dreams,

* Page 162.   † Page 163.

‡ " Among the Hills ; " Poetical Works, i., 260. It is fair to add that this extract is from the Prelude.

Confesses it.   The locust by the wall
Stabs the noon-silence with his sharp alarm.
A single hay-cart down the dusty road
Creaks slowly, with its driver fast asleep
On the load's top.   Against the neighboring hill,
Huddled along the stone-wall's shady side,
The sheep show white, as if a snow-drift still
Defied the dog-star.   Through the open door
A drowsy smell of flowers—gray heliotrope,
And white sweet clover, and shy mignonette—
Comes faintly in, and silent chorus lends
To the prevailing symphony of peace."

Everywhere in Whittier's work one may find
such pictures. Quite to appreciate them, perhaps, one must know the country they deal with.
The regions of New England that Whittier knew
have a character peculiarly their own. The rocky
coast between Cape Ann and the Piscataqua,
broken by long stretches of beach; the marshes,
dotted with great stacks of salt hay, stretching
back to the woods or the farms of the solid land;
the rolling country, with its elms and pines, its
gnarled apple-orchards, its gray wooden farm-
houses; and almost within sight the lower spurs
of the New Hampshire hills, bristling with a
stubble of young woods, are unlike any other
country I know. Such subtile impressions as
mark the individuality of a region are unmis-
takable, but almost beyond the power of words to
phrase. Perhaps the trait which most distinguishes this country that Whittier so knew and

12

loved, is a nearer approach to the suggestion of a romantic past than is common in North America. Far as the eye can reach or the foot travel, this region has been the home of our own race for above two centuries. It has its own traditions, its own legends. It is humanized in a way almost European. Yet its legends and its traditions belong to a past not of civilized or mediæval grandeur, but of savage wildness. And its actual prosperity is past or passing—but for great factories, swarming with foreign operatives, or for summer visitors who come to idle in the regions where the toil of the past generations bred the race that has tamed a savage continent.

In these regions it was Whittier's lot to know the last days of the olden time and the first of the new. He loved the old days for their hardy virtues ; his faith in human nature, always guided by the inner light, allowed him no misgivings for the future. In "Cobbler Keezar's Vision," * the German wizard finds the Merrimac of the future, with its scores of mill-wheels, and its white-walled farm-houses, and its floating flags of freedom, a lovelier sight than his memories of the vine-clad Rhine, with its clowns and puppets, its flagons and its despotism. Whittier found the Merrimac lovelier himself—a task in which he was probably helped by the narrow limits of his

* Poetical Works, i., 241.

travels. He loved the Nature about him. He found in it something which constantly rewarded and strengthened his life-long love.

Expressing this constant delight in the country that his verses have made peculiarly his own, he accomplished, half unwittingly, the work which in all likelihood will ultimately be thought his best. One may question, if one choose, the merit of his personal and religious poems ; one may find his romantic narratives trivial, and his passionate advocacy of reform blind, dangerous, truculent ; but one cannot deny that he has seen the landscapes of his own New England with an eye as searching as it was loving, or that he has told us what he saw so simply, so truly, so constantly that, however time or chance may change in years to come the face of the regions he knew so well, the things he saw and loved may be seen and loved throughout time by all who will but read. The peculiar character of his poetry of Nature is that it is not interpretative but faithfully representative. The examples of it already quoted are enough to show this trait. There are critics, then, and real lovers of poetry, who find his work harshly literal, unimaginative, prosaic. Such critics, I think, will not let themselves sympathize with the exquisitely sympathetic sense of fact which underlies his utter simplicity. When he tried to interpret, he added nothing to his work. When he was content to tell us what he saw, he showed us constantly what many of us should never have seen for ourselves ; and this he showed so truly that, as in the course of centuries proves true of the art which the centuries pronounce great, each one of us may in turn interpret it anew for himself, just as each may interpret for himself the life that passes before his living eyes.

IX

In this constant strength of his instinctive fidelity to Nature, Whittier distinguishes himself from almost all other American men of letters.   In most of our literature there is a quality of consciousness.   Sometimes this takes the form of aggressive cleverness ; sometimes it deliberately assumes the traditional dignity of culture ; often — and perhaps most characteristically—it half-consciously, half-unwittingly follows or revives tradition.   As somebody has extravagantly said, American verse swarms with nightingales— a bird unknown on this continent.   For this state of things there is a reason which these perhaps imaginary nightingales typify.   An American would not be a true son of the fathers if he did not instinctively love tradition.   The emigrants brought from the Old World fireside tales of things and folks, of pomps and grandeurs, of comedies and tragedies which their children could never know in the flesh.   And history has moved fast with us, and society has been overturned more than once.   And Western children to-day are listening to such stories of New England as Yankee children of the early days heard about Old England itself.   This love of tradition, which shows itself perhaps most markedly in the passion for genealogy which permeates New England, is a prime trait of the true Yankee.   Whittier was as true a Yankee as ever lived.   His first published volume, we remember, was a volume of "New England Legends."   New England legends he continued to write almost all his life ; and, as his reading extended, he wrote many other legends, too, of regions and races that he had never known in the flesh.

Of the latter little need be said.   They are not profoundly characteristic.   He got them from books, and he put them into other books, where their simple ballad-form makes them pleasantly readable.   He generally managed to infuse into them a certain amount of blameless moralizing which does not enhance their stimulating quality.   On the whole, we may class them with that great body of innocuous American verse which is permeated with the innocent unreality of conscious culture.

The New England legends are of firmer stuff. In his prose works one finds some of the material that goes to make them.   "Charms and Fairy

Faith," and "Magicians and Witch Folk " * tell of such actual traditions as were kept alive at the snow-bound fireside. "Margaret Smith's Journal," † while no permanent contribution to historical fiction, is so true a picture of the Seventeenth Century in New England as to prove beyond peradventure the solidity of Whittier's study in local history. And verses like these ‡ show how well he knew the ancestral Puritans :

" With the memory of that morning by the summer sea I
  blend
 A wild and wondrous story, by the younger Mather
  penned,
 In that quaint *Magnalia Christi*, with all strange and
  marvellous things,
 Heaped up huge and undigested, like the chaos Ovid
  sings.

" Dear to me these far, faint glimpses of the dual life of
  old,
 Inward, grand with awe and reverence ; outward, mean
  and coarse and cold ;
 Gleams of mystic beauty playing over dull and vulgar
  clay,
 Golden-threaded fancies weaving in a web of hodden
  gray."

His romantic and legendary narratives of New England, then, have much of the true flavour of

* Prose Works, i., 385, 399.   † Ibid., 9.
‡ " The Garrison of Cape Ann ; " Poetical Works, i., 166.

the soil.   He seems to have been haunted, however, by a lurking Yankee conscience which constantly suggested doubts as to whether it is quite
right to tell a good story just for its own sake.
His introduction to the " Tent on the Beach," *
the volume which contained, on the whole, his
most effective narrative poems, is distinctly apol-
ogetic.   Here, at fifty-nine, he writes :

> " I would not sin in this half-playful strain,—
>   Too light perhaps for serious years, though born
> Of the enforced leisure of slow pain,—
>   Against the pure ideal which has drawn
> My feet to follow its far-shining gleam."

As a result of this state of things, his narratives
of New England tradition generally deal with
such phases of it as have perceptible didactic significance.   Naturally, he represents the Quakers
heroically.   A typical stanza is this, from the
"King's Missive," written at seventy-two : †

> " 'Off with the knave's hat ! '   An angry hand
>   Smote down the offence ; but the wearer said,
> With a quiet smile, ' By the king's command
>   I bear his message and stand in his stead.'
> In the Governor's hand a missive he laid
>   With the royal arms on its seal displayed,

* Poetical Works, iv., 227.
† Ibid., i., 383.   We must remember that Quaker principles forbade salutation by uncovering the head.

> And the proud man spake as he glanced thereat,
> Uncovering, 'Give Mr. Shattuck his hat.'"

Indubitably didactic in motive, too, are those two narrative poems of his which are apparently most familiar : " Maud Muller," * written at forty-six ; and " Skipper Ireson's Ride," † written at forty-nine. The merits and the limits of his work in this kind are patent in " Maud Muller." The little poem is very simple, and in its conventional sentimentality is very acceptable to the great American public. In its presentation of a Yankee judge in the character of a knightly hero of romance, it is artlessly consonant with the social ideals of the Yankee country ; so, too, in its tacit assumption that the good looks of a barefoot country beauty would really have been more congenial life-companions in an eminent legal career than the rich dower and the fashionable tendencies of the lady whom the Judge ultimately married in deference to

> " his sisters proud and cold,
> And his mother, vain of her rank and gold."

If this sort of thing were canting, it would be abominable. What saves it is that it rings true. The man meant it seriously. We may smile at his simplicity, if we like; but we can hardly help loving him for it. Indeed, it is almost

---

* Poetical Works, i., 148.   † Ibid., 174.

enough to make us forgive that insidiously dreadful rhyme—

> " For of all sad words of tongue or pen,
>   The saddest are these : ' It might have been ! ' "

"Skipper Ireson's Ride," on the other hand,
has much of the true ballad quality :

> " Body of turkey, head of owl,
>   Wings a-droop like a rained-on fowl,
>   Feathered and ruffled in every part,
>   Skipper Ireson stood in the cart.
>   Scores of women, old and young,
>   Strong of muscle and glib of tongue,
>   Pushed and pulled up the rocky lane,
>   Shouting and singing the shrill refrain :
>   ' Here's Flud Oirson, fur his horrd horrt,
>   Torr'd an' futherr'd an' corr'd in a corrt
>   By the women o' Morble'ead ! ' "

Such a subject as this stirred the Yankee
Quaker to the depths. A human being, deaf to
the still small voice, had acted devilishly. The
weakest creatures of his seaside home had ris-
en up against him ; and, not overstepping the
bounds of due punishment, had held him up lastingly to public scorn and detestation. It is perhaps instructive, in connection with such reforming enthusiasm as pervades this spirited ballad,
to learn from a note in the final edition * that,
twenty-two years after the original publication,

* Poetical Works, i., 174.

Whittier was credibly informed that Ireson had really been innocent. Against the skipper's will, it appeared, his refractory crew had compelled him to desert his sinking townsfolk; and then, to screen themselves, they had falsely accused him, with the direful result commemorated by the poet. His answer to his informant is characteristic :

> "I have now no doubt that thy version of Skipper Ireson's ride is the correct one. My verse was founded solely on a fragment of rhyme which I heard from one of my early schoolmates, a native of Marblehead.
>
> "I supposed the story to which it referred dated back at least a century. I knew nothing of the participators, and the narrative of the ballad was pure fancy. I am glad for the sake of truth and justice that the real facts are given in thy book. I certainly would not knowingly do injustice to any one, dead or living."

And having thus, introductorily, done full justice to the memory of poor Floyd Ireson, he proceeds to reprint his ballad.

In touching these narrative and legendary poems of Whittier, I have perhaps allowed myself to lay undue emphasis on phases of them that are not their best. One and all of them we may certainly call simple, earnest, artless, and beautifully true to the native traditions and temper of New England. In that last fact, however, which I have tried to emphasize, lies their weakness as literature. The temper of New England is essentially serious, always uncomfortable if it cannot defend itself on firm ethical grounds. Thoroughly good narrative, on the other hand, ought to be as free from obvious ethical admixture as are the exquisitely pure descriptions of New England landscape, which seem to me Whittier's most lasting work. At times these narratives of his blend almost inextricably with his poems of Nature; from the narratives may be selected extracts which, in simple descriptive power, are as beautiful as anything Whittier ever did. In general, however, the impression that these narratives make is one of saturation with the traditional ethical ideals of New England, curiously combined with that constant reliance on inner inspiration toward the Right which is the fundamental tenet of the Quaker faith. All men are really equal, he assumes throughout, all ought to be really free; let them be free, and all they have to do is to follow the inner light. And here these narrative poems touch close, on the other hand, the works which Whittier deemed his best—his works for reform. A passage like this, which closes the "King's Missive," * might have belonged to either class :

> "The Puritan spirit perishing not,
>   To Concord's yeomen the signal sent,
> And spake in the voice of the cannon-shot
>   That severed the chains of a continent.

* Poetical Works, i., 386.

With its gentler message of peace and good-will
The thought of the Quaker is living still,
And the freedom of soul he prophesied
Is gospel and law where the martyrs died."

X

From beginning to end, Whittier was an honest champion of human freedom. We have seen enough of the peculiar religious faith from which he never swerved, to understand how inevitable such a position must have seemed to him. We have seen enough of his own almost childlike simplicity and honesty of temperament to understand the whole-souled, unhesitating vigour with which he threw himself into the task to which he felt himself called. To every human being, he believed, God has given the inner light. Leave human beings free to act, then, as God meant them to act, and God's will shall be done. The voice of the people is literally the voice of God; it is the concrete, numerical expression of the whisperings of the still small voice. Whether the human form to which the voice whispers be European, Asiatic, African, or American, makes no manner of difference. Difference of race is merely a variety of complexion; a majority of negroes is as divinely true a force as a majority of Puritan farmers. Are not all alike made in God's image, all alike human, all alike accessible to the inner light and the still small voice which can lead only toward the Truth? Admit such premises—and Whittier never for a moment doubted them—and there is room for only one conclusion : Whatever opposes any form of human freedom is against God's will. Not to proclaim this truth—not to assert it in every word and deed—is to be what Whittier could never have been, a deliberate coward.

In the course of his life he advocated more reforms than one. His conduct in regard to the abolition of slavery, however, is typical of his conduct throughout. It will serve our purpose to consider that alone.

Quite to appreciate the courage implied in the public assertion of anti-slavery opinions sixty years ago demands to-day no small effort of imagination. It was far greater than that which would be shown to-day by an ambitious aspirant for public honours who should honestly and openly question the wisdom of the ultimate abolition of slavery. To-day such an opinion, which was the dominant opinion in 1830, could result in no worse harm than political ridicule or neglect. It would hardly diminish the number or the cordiality of one's social invitations. In 1830 an Abolitionist was held little less than treasonable. Social ostracism was almost certainly his due. His very person was not safe from public attack ; and the blind hostility of the mob—which for some years to come was far too noisy to detect the

whisperings of any still small voice—was confirmed by that profoundly honest belief in the
public duty of maintaining existing institutions
which has always characterized the better classes
in any community of British origin.   Perhaps the
closest analogy which we can imagine to-day to
the Abolitionists of 1833 would be a body of
earnest, God-fearing men who should be convinced that God bade them cry out against the
institution of marriage.

In the face of such a state of public opinion as
this, Whittier never for a moment faltered. He
knew he was right. The one curse spared him
was the curse of even momentary doubt. Shy in
temperament, loving most of all the simple seclu-
sion of his native country, he never hesitated to
speak and to act with all his power for the cause
of human freedom. That enfranchisement, in the
broadest sense, could possibly result only in a
new phase of evil, he never dreamt to the end.
He was a man. Negroes, Indians, Chinamen,
Polish Jews, are men, too. Let all have equal
rights, all an equal voice, all be equal in the sight
of man as they are eternally equal in the sight of
God.

What he actually did we have seen in our
brief record of his life. That brief record has been
enough to show that the dreadful fact of slavery
was a fact of which he had little direct knowledge. He was at Washington in 1845. Apart

from that his knowledge of actual slaves must have been derived chiefly from fugitives, whose versions of their experience must wholly have confirmed his most extreme views. But what mattered that? When one knows a thing evil, one need not study it in detail to know that right and justice demand its extinction. From such fanatical, heroic logic there is no escape. We have seen, I said, what his actual conduct was. For thirty years and more his words supported, defended, urged on such lines of conduct. Occasionally, in his own phrase,*

> " The cant of party, school, and sect,
>   Provoked at times his honest scorn,
> And Folly, in its gray respect,
>   He tossed on satire's horn."

As we have seen, though, he lacked humour or wit to make his satire really powerful or trenchant. His words that really did their work, the words that still tell the story of the great public movement in which he was a foremost figure, were those simple, passionate utterances that came straight from his heart.

There is room here to quote only a few. But a very few should suffice to give some taste of the quality of all.

At twenty-six he wrote, for the meeting of

* Poetical Works, ii., 120.

the Anti-Slavery Society in New York, a hymn.*
Here are a few stanzas :

> " When from each temple of the free,
>   A nation's voice ascends to Heaven,
>   Most Holy Father! unto Thee
>   May not our humble prayer be given ?

> " Thy children all, though hue and form
>   Are varied in Thine own good will,
>   With Thy own holy breathings warm,
>   And fashioned in Thine image still.

> .   .   .   .   .   .

> " For broken heart, and clouded mind,
>   Whereon no human mercies fall ;
>   Oh, be Thy gracious love inclined,
>   Who, as a Father, pitiest all !

> " And grant, O Father ! that the time
>   Of Earth's deliverance may be near,
>   When every land and tongue and clime
>   The message of Thy love shall hear."

At twenty-eight, when resolutions had been
adopted in Congress forbidding the postal cir-
culation of anti-slavery literature, he wrote a
" Summons "† to the North.   Here is a touch of
its quality :

> " Methinks from all her wild, green mountains ;
>   From valleys where her slumbering fathers lie ;
>   From her blue rivers and her welling fountains,
>   And clear, cold sky ;

* Poetical Works, iii., 29.   † Ibid., 40.

" From her rough coast and isles, which hungry Ocean
    Gnaws with his surges ; from the fisher's skiff,
With white sail swaying to the billows' motion
    Round rock and cliff ;

"From the free fireside of her unbought farmer ;
    From her free laborer at his loom and wheel ;
From the brown smith-shop, where, beneath the hammer,
    Rings the red steel ;

" From each and all, if God hath not forsaken
    Our land, and left us to an evil choice,
Loud as the summer thunderbolt shall waken
    A People's voice.

"Startling and stern ! the Northern winds shall bear it
    Over Potomac's to St. Mary's wave ;
And buried Freedom shall awake to hear it
    Within her grave."

At thirty-five he wrote the passionate address,
"Massachusetts to Virginia," * concerning the
seizure in Boston of one Latimer, a fugitive
slave. To appreciate its stirring vigour one
should read it all. But here is a bit of it :

" From Norfolk's ancient villages, from Plymouth's rocky
    bound
  To where Nantucket feels the arms of ocean close her
    round ;

" From rich and rural Worcester, where through the calm
    repose
  Of cultured vales and fringing woods the gentle Nashua
    flows,

       * Poetical Works, iii., 80.

13

To where Wachuset's wintry blasts the mountain larches
    stir,
Swelled up to Heaven the thrilling cry of 'God save
    Latimer!'

" And sandy Barnstable rose up, wet with the salt sea
    spray;
And Bristol sent her answering shout down Narragansett
    Bay!
Along the broad Connecticut old Hampden felt the thrill,
And the cheer of Hampshire's woodmen swept down from
    Holyoke Hill.

" The voice of Massachusetts! Of her free sons and daugh-
    ters,
Deep calling unto deep aloud, the sound of many waters!
Against the burden of that voice what tyrant power shall
    stand?
No fetters in the Bay State! No slave upon her land!"

At forty-nine, when the elections of 1856 had
shown the gains of the Free-Soil party, he wrote
this: *

        " For God be praised! New England
           Takes once more her ancient place;
        Again the Pilgrim's banner
           Leads the vanguard of the race.

      .   .   .   .

        " The Northern hills are blazing,
           The Northern skies are bright;
        The fair young West is turning
           Her forehead to the light!
      .   .   .   .

      * " A Song; " Poetical Works, iii., 192.

> " Push every outpost nearer,
>   Press hard the hostile towers !
> Another Balaklava,
>   And the Malakoff is ours ! "

The tide was turning. Four years later came
the war. Here is a bit of his first war poem : *

> " We see not, know not ; all our way
>   Is night—with Thee alone is day :
>   From out the torrent's troubled drift,
>   Above the storm our prayers we lift,
>   Thy will be done !
>
> .   .   .   .
>
> " Strike, Thou the Master, we Thy keys,
>   The anthem of the destinies !
>   The minor of Thy loftier strain,
>   Our hearts shall breathe the old refrain,
>   Thy will be done ! "

" Barbara Frietchie " † every one knows —perhaps the most instantly popular ballad of the
war. " Laus Deo ! " ‡ in celebration of the con-
stitutional abolition of slavery, is not so familiar.
Every word of that should be read, too. Here
are a few :

> " It is done !
> Clang of bell and roar of gun
> Send the tidings up and down.
>   How the belfries rock and reel !
>   How the great guns, peal on peal,
> Fling the joy from town to town !
>
> .   .   .   .

* "Thy Will be Done ; " Poetical Works, iii., 217.
† Poetical Works, iii., 245.   ‡ Ibid., 254.

"Did we dare,
In our agony of prayer,
Ask for more than He has done ?
When was ever His right hand
Over any time or land
Stretched as now beneath the sun ?

.   .   .   .

"Ring and swing,
Bells of joy ! On morning's wing
Send the song of praise abroad !
With a sound of broken chains
Tell the nations that He reigns,
Who alone is Lord and God !"

These few extracts must suffice to represent
the most earnest work he did for above thirty
years. With more intensity, with genuine passion, they show the same sincerity, the same simplicity that we have felt in him throughout.
And he knew the rare happiness of complete conquest. Beginning with all the world against him,
he found himself for the last twenty years of his
life in a world where all were against his foes.

XI

In view of this, we may well pause to consider
two extracts from his writings—one in prose and
one in verse—without which our impression of
him would be seriously incomplete. They show
that he possessed the power which is perhaps the
test of manly greatness—the power of serenely

recognizing the worth of men from whom for years he honestly and passionately differed.

The first is from a letter of regret that he could not attend a meeting in memory of Edward Everett : *

" When the grave closed over him who added new lustre to the old and honoured name of Quincy, all eyes instinctively turned to Edward Everett as the last of that venerated class of patriotic civilians who, outliving all dissent and jealousy and party prejudice, held their reputation by the secure tenure of the universal appreciation of its worth as a common treasure of the republic.   It is not for me to pronounce his eulogy.   . . . My secluded country life has afforded me few opportunities of personal intercourse with him, while my pronounced radicalism on the great question which has divided popular feeling rendered our political paths widely divergent.   Both of us early saw the danger which threatened the country.   . . . But while he believed in the possibility of averting it by concession and compromise, I, on the contrary, as firmly believed that such a course could only strengthen and confirm what I regarded as a gigantic conspiracy against the rights and liberties, the union and the life, of the nation.   . . .

" Recent events have certainly not tended to change this belief on my part; but in looking over the past, while I see little or nothing to retract in the matter of opinion, I am saddened by the reflection that through the very intensity of my convictions I may have done injustice to the motives of those with whom I differed.   As respects Edward Everett, it seems to me that only within the last four years † I have truly known him."

* Prose Works, ii., 274.   Written in 1865.

† These, we must remember, were the years of the war.

Fifteen years before he wrote this letter, he had written concerning Webster's Seventh-of-March Speech the scathing invective which he named " Ichabod : " *

> " So fallen ! so lost ! the light withdrawn
>   Which once he wore !
> The glory from his grey hairs gone
>   For evermore !
>
> .   .   .   .
>
> " Let not the land once proud of him
>   Insult him now,
> Nor brand with deeper shame the dim,
>   Dishonoured brow.
>
> " But let its humbled sons, instead,
>   From sea to lake,
> A long lament, as for the dead,
>   In sadness make.
>
> .   .   .   .
>
> " Then pay the reverence of old days
>   To his dead fame ;
> Walk backward, with averted gaze,
>   And hide the shame ! "

Fifteen years after Edward Everett's death, and thirty years after this " Ichabod " had seen the light, Whittier wrote of Webster once more.   In his collected works he departs for once from chronology, and puts beside " Ichabod " his final poem on Webster—the " Lost Occasion : " †

* Poetical Works, iv., 62.   † Ibid., 63.

" Thou shouldst have lived to feel below
   Thy feet Disunion's fierce upthrow ;
   The late-sprung mine that underlaid
   Thy sad concessions vainly made.
   Thou shouldst have seen from Sumter's wall
   The star-flag of the Union fall,
   And armed rebellion pressing on
   The broken lines of Washington !
   No stronger voice than thine had then
   Called out the utmost might of men,
   To make the Union's charter free
   And strengthen law by liberty.

    .   .   .   .

   Wise men and strong we did not lack ;
   But still, with memory turning back,
   In the dark hours we thought of thee,
   And thy lone grave beside the sea.

    .   .   .   .   .   .

   But, where thy native mountains bare
   Their foreheads to diviner air,
   Fit emblem of enduring fame,
   One lofty summit keeps thy name.
   For thee the cosmic forces did
   The rearing of that pyramid,
   The prescient ages shaping with
   Fire, flood, and frost thy monolith.
   Sunrise and sunset lay thereon
   With hands of light their benison,
   The stars of midnight pause to set
   Their jewels in its coronet.
   And evermore that mountain mass
   Seems climbing from the shadowy pass
   To light, as if to manifest
   Thy nobler self, thy life at best ! "

Is it too much to see in these lines not an assent but an approach to that view of the Seventh-of-March Speech which some, of the younger generation, are beginning to take? that it may have been not what men thought it at the time—a blind sacrifice of principle to self; but rather the most nobly patriotic act of a nobly patriotic career—a deliberate sacrifice of self to the Union which without such sacrifice was not yet strong enough to survive?

XII

But this is not the place for political speculation. I have tried to show Whittier as he was, extenuating nothing nor setting down aught in malice. Above most men, he was one who can stand the test. His faults are patent. One cannot read him long without forgetting them in admiration of his nobly simple merits. Before considering his work in detail, I suggested that his chance of survival is better than that of any other contemporary American man of letters. Our consideration of his work has perhaps shown why. In the first place, he has recorded in a way as yet unapproached the homely beauties of New England Nature. In the second, he accepted with all his heart the traditional democratic principles of equality and freedom which have always animated the people of New England. These principles he uttered in words whose simplicity goes straight to the hearts of the whole American people. Whether these principles be true or false is no concern of ours here. If our republic is to live, they are the principles which must prevail. And in the verses of Whittier they are preserved to guide posterity, in the words of one who was incapable of falsehood.

VII

MR. LOWELL AS A TEACHER

[Published in *Scribner's Magazine*, November, 1891.]

MR. LOWELL AS A TEACHER

I

As a student in Harvard College during the years 1876 and 1877—the last two years of Mr. Lowell's regular teaching there—I had the fortune to be his pupil. My memories of him, in a character not generally known, are perhaps worth recording.

II

In my Junior year, a lecture of Professor Norton's excited in me a wish to read Dante under Mr. Lowell. I did not know a word of Italian, though; and I was firmly resolved to waste no more time on elementary grammar. Without much hope of a favourable reception, then, I applied for admission to the course. Mr. Lowell received me in one of the small recitation-rooms in the upper story of University Hall. My first impression was that he was surprisingly hirsute, and a little eccentric in aspect. He wore a double-breasted sack-coat, by no means new. In his necktie, which was tied in a sailor-knot, was a pin—an article of adornment at that time recently condemned by an authority which some of us were then disposed to accept as gospel. On his desk lay a silk hat not lately brushed; and nobody, I then held, had any business to wear a silk hat unless he wore coat-tails, too.

My second impression, which was fixed the moment he looked at me, and which has never altered, was that I had never met anybody quite so quizzical. Naturally I was not exactly at ease; and Mr. Lowell appeared to take a repressed but boyish delight in keeping me a bit uneasy. He listened to my application kindly, though; and finally, with a gesture that I remember as very like a stretch, told me to come in to the course and see what I could do with Dante.

To that time my experience of academic teaching had led me to the belief that the only way to study a classic text in any language was to scrutinize every syllable with a care undisturbed by consideration of any more of the context than was grammatically related to it. Any real reading I had done, I had had to do without a teacher. Mr. Lowell never gave us less than a canto to read; and often gave us two or three. He never, from the beginning, bothered us with a particle of linguistic irrelevance. Here before us was a great poem—a lasting expression of what human life had meant to a human being, dead and gone these five centuries. Let us try, as best we might, to see what life had meant to this man;

let us see what relation his experience, great and
small, bore to ours; and, now and then, let us
pause for a moment to notice how wonderfully
beautiful his expression of this experience was.
Let us read, as sympathetically as we could make
ourselves read, the words of one who was as much
a man as we ; only vastly greater in his knowledge
of wisdom and of beauty. That was the spirit of
Mr. Lowell's teaching. It opened to some of us
a new world. In a month, I could read Dante
better than I ever learned to read Greek, or Latin,
or German.

His method of teaching was all his own. The
class was small—not above ten or a dozen; and
he generally began by making each student translate a few lines, interrupting now and then with
suggestions of the poetic value of passages which
were being rendered in a style too exasperatingly
prosaic. Now and again, some word or some passage would suggest to him a line of thought—
sometimes very earnest, sometimes paradoxically
comical—that it would never have suggested to
anyone else. And he would lean back in his
chair, and talk away across country till he felt
like stopping; or he would thrust his hands into
the pockets of his rather shabby sack-coat, and
pace the end of the room with his heavy laced
boots, and look at nothing in particular, and discourse of things in general. We gave up note-
books in a week. Our business was not to cram

lifeless detail, but to absorb as much as we might
of the spirit of his exuberant literary vitality.
And through it all he was always a quiz; you
never knew what he was going to do or to say
next. One whimsical digression I have always
remembered, chiefly for the amiable atrocity of
the pun. Some mention of wings had been made
in the text, whereupon Mr. Lowell observed that
he had always had a liking for wings: he had
lately observed that some were being added to the
ugliest house in Cambridge, and he cherished
hopes that they might fly away with it. I remember, too, how one tremendous passage in the
"Inferno" started him off in a disquisition concerning canker-worms, and other less mentionable
—if more diverting—vermin. And then, all of a
sudden, he soared up into the clouds, and pounced
down on the text again, and asked the next man
to translate. You could not always be sure when
he was in earnest; but there was never a moment
when he let you forget that you were a human being in a human world, and that Dante had been
one, too. One or two of us, among ourselves,
nicknamed him "sweet wag;" I like the name
still.

After a month or two, he found that we were
not advancing fast enough. So he fell into a way
of making us read one canto to him, and then
reading the next to us. If we wished to interrupt
him, we were as free to do so as he was to inter-

rupt us. There was one man in the class, I remember, who liked to read out-of-the-way books, and who used to break in on Mr. Lowell's translation with questions about Gabriel Harvey and other such worthies, rather humorously copying Mr. Lowell's own irrelevancies; but he could never get hold of anything so out of the way that Mr. Lowell had not read it, or at least could not talk about it as easily as if he had read it often. So, in a single college year, we read through the Divine Comedy, and the Vita Nuova; and dipped into the Convito and the lesser writings of Dante. And more than one of us learned to love them always.

III

THIS class-room work, however, was to some of us the least important part of Mr. Lowell's teaching. Almost as soon as the year began, he announced that he should always be at home one evening in the week, and glad to see us. Several of us took him at his word, and even took his word to signify more than the good man ever meant it to. For if the evening he set aside for us proved inconvenient, we made no scruple of going to Elmwood at other times; and if Mr. Lowell was at home—as he generally was in those years—we were always admitted.

It is those evenings with him in his library that one remembers best. There was always a wood-fire burning above a bed of ashes which had been accumulating for years. He would generally sit at one side of the fire, within easy reach of the tongs, which he often plied as he talked. What is more, when some of us grew more familiar and ventured to ply the tongs ourselves, he would not interfere. He would always be rather carelessly dressed: a loose smoking-jacket, I think, and often slippers. And he would smoke a pipe. He would generally begin the evening by offering one a cigar. My impression, I remember, was that the cigar was always the same, and for some months I did not dare accept it. Finally, I summoned courage to smoke it, and found it very dry and the wrapper cracked; which went far to confirm my impression. But one did not care about that sort of thing. His pipe fairly started, Mr. Lowell would begin to talk, in his own quizzical way—at one moment beautifully in earnest, at the next so whimsical that you could not quite make out what he meant—about whatever came into his head. It might be what he had just been reading; he had generally just been reading some bit of old literature—once I remember finding him deep in a narrative in the Apocrypha, which he went on reading aloud. It might be the news of the day, it might be reminiscence of any kind. All we had to do was to sit and listen, which was far better than any other way of spending an evening known to me in those days. To talk to him was

hard. A man to whom people have liked to listen these thirty years rarely remains a good listener to things like undergraduate chatter, which
are not worth serious attention. But when he did
listen, and when he talked, too, he did so—no
matter how quizzically—with a certain politeness
that at the time seemed to me, and in memory remains, a typical example of the signification of
the word *urbane;* and all this in smoking-jacket
and slippers, by lamp-light, before a flickering
wood-fire whose ashes were crumbling down into a
great bed which had grown from hundreds of such
fires before.

The human friendliness of those evenings, whoever knew them cannot forget. To some of us it
gave a new meaning to everything he touched, in
teaching or in talk. Here was a man who faced
great things and little undismayed; who found
in literature not something gravely mysterious,
but only the best record that human beings have
made of human life ; who found, too, in human
life—old and new—not something to be disdained
with the serene contempt of smug scholarship,
but the everlasting material from which literature
and art are made. Here was a man, you grew to
feel, who knew literature, and knew the world,
and knew you, too ; ready and willing, in a
friendly way, to speak the word of cordial introduction. There came from those evenings a certain feeling of personal affection for him, very

rare in any student's experience of even the most faithful teacher.

Yet, faithful as his work was in spirit, he hated the details of it, and sometimes treated them with a whimsical disregard that whoever did not appreciate how thoroughly it put them where they belonged might have deemed cynically indifferent. I remember an example of this in connection with an examination—I believe the first he gave us. There are few things less favourable to literary culture than written examinations; they are almost unmitigated, if quite necessary, evils. Perhaps from unwillingness to degrade the text of Dante to such use, Mr. Lowell set us, when we had read the Inferno and part of the Purgatorio, a paper consisting of nothing but a long passage from Massimo d' Azeglio, which we had three hours to translate. This task we performed as best we might. Weeks passed, and no news came of our marks. At last one of the class, who was not quite at ease concerning his academic standing, ventured, at the close of a recitation, to ask if Mr. Lowell had assigned him a mark. Mr. Lowell looked at the youth very gravely, and inquired what he really thought his work deserved. The student rather diffidently said that he hoped it was worth sixty per cent. "You may take it," said Mr. Lowell; "and I shan't have the bother of reading your book."

I remember two or three instances of the curious friendliness which by and by sprang up between him and his pupils. At that time the students were publishing a paper which contained likenesses of the faculty, imitated—at the longest of intervals—from *Vanity Fair*. When a portrait of Mr. Lowell appeared, with his sack-coat, and his silk hat, and his heavy boots all duly emphasised, somebody ventured to ask him how he liked it. To which he replied that he had been grieved to observe that the artist had allowed a handkerchief to protrude from his breast-pocket; but had been consoled by the fact that the artist had kindly permitted him to wear plaid trousers —an innocent fancy of his to which Mrs. Lowell strongly objected.

Another, very different, example of his way of treating us appeared one evening, when I went alone to call at Elmwood, and found him alone in his library. I had never seen him so stern in aspect, so absent in manner. In a moment he told me why. He had just heard of the death of a dear friend. Of course I rose to go, but he detained me; it would do him good, he said, to talk. I have always wished that I had written down what I remembered of the talk that followed, for it still seems to me that I have never heard another so memorable; but all that remains with me now is the very beginning. There is one blessed comfort, he said, that comes with death; then, at last, we can begin, with cer-

tainty of no awaking disenchantment, to idealise
those we love. It is the dead, unbodied Beatrice
who lives for ever in the lines of Dante. We can
watch among our friends the growth of their own
Beatrices that such as have had the happiness to
know them make amid the agonies of bereave-
ment, each for himself. This friend of his own,
just dead, was already gathering to herself the unmixed glories of the ideality which would gather
about her as long as those who loved her should
live to know it.—And so he talked on, rambling
far and wide, not forgetting now and then the
whimsicality without which his talk would not
have been his, nor ever forgetting either the deep
gravity of the mood in which I had found him.
That talk was such a poem as I have never read.
When at last I left him, he took my hand more
warmly than ever before. It had done him good,
that silent greeting said, to talk, to have any
listener.

The feeling of personal regard which came from
such intercourse as this was different from anything else I knew as a student. You felt, at last,
in spite of all his quizzical whimsicality, a sen-
timent of intimacy, of confidence, of familiarity
which no one else excited. You felt instinctively
that such a feeling must be mutual. Mr. Lowell
was a celebrated man, of course ; a serious figure
in American literature. But at that moment,
though he was still in the full vigour of life, his

work seemed pretty well over. You thought of him as a kind old friend, resting contemplatively before his wood-fire, thinking and talking of all manner of human things; and waiting, very serenely, in sack-coat and slippers, for the far-off end of an ideal life of letters. It was just at the end of my second year of study with him—a year in which he had taught me almost as much over the text of Roland and other dreary old French poems as he had taught over Dante himself— that the news came that he was going to Spain.

IV

I HEARD it, I think, on our Class-Day. The class had distinguished itself by an internal squabble which had prevented the election of Class-Day officers, and consequently the usual oration and poem, and so on. By way of peace-making, perhaps, Mr. Lowell had invited us all to an open-air breakfast at Elmwood, at the hour when formal ceremonies usually make the beginning of Class-Day at Harvard so remote from amusing. Few of the men knew him, even by sight; but all found him so cordial a host that for the moment our animosities were half forgotten. I asked him if the report of his mission were true; and he said it was. I remember wondering how this friendly, careless, whimsical, human man of letters, who had seemed so perma-

nently settled in his arm-chair, would manage the
rather serious business of diplomatic life; wondering, with true boyish impudence, whether he
would be up to it.   After that day I did not see
him until his final return from the mission to
England.

All the time I had felt as if such intimate personal feeling as he had aroused and permitted
must have been mutual.   When at last I met him
again, it was a slight shock to find that he had
quite forgotten my face, and almost forgotten
my name.   The truth was, I began at last to see,
that throughout those old days he had known
better than any of us what dull, fruitless beings
we college boys were; but that his business
had been to teach us all he could, and he had
known that he, at least, could teach best by show-
ing himself to us as he was.   All this kindness,
all this friendliness, all this humanity was real;
all the culture he had striven to impart to us was
as precious as we had ever thought it.   We ourselves, though, were mere passing figures, not
worth very serious personal memory; and Mr.
Lowell valued people at their true worth, and was
beautifully free from that clerical kind of humbug
which presses your hand after an interval of years,
and asks feelingly for the dear children it has
never bothered its wits about.   And the fact that
all he had been to us and all he had done for us
had been his honest, earnest work as a teacher,

and not his spontaneous conduct as a human being, makes it seem now all the more admirable.
I have often shuddered to think how we must
have bored him ; I have never ceased more and
more to admire the faithful persistency with
which he inspired us.

The last time I spoke to him was on his seven-
tieth birthday. A public dinner had been given
him, and in the speeches his public life and
works had been rehearsed from beginning to end ;
but not a word had been said of his teaching.
After dinner I told him that this omission had
meant much to me, that to me he would always
be chiefly the most inspiring teacher I had ever
had. His face lighted with the old quizzical
smile, and I could not tell quite how much he
was in earnest when, with all the old urbanity, he
answered : "I'm glad you said that. I've been
wondering if I hadn't wasted half my life."

www.ingramcontent.com/pod-product-compliance
Lightning Source LLC
Chambersburg PA
CBHW021437020726
47499CB00006BA/2039